永恆的莎士比亞改寫劇本❹

馬克白

MACBETH

William Shakespeare ◆ 著

Brady Timoney ◆ 改寫 ｜ 蘇瑞琴 ◆ 譯

MP3

永恆的莎士比亞改寫劇本 ❹
馬克白
MACBETH

作　　者	William Shakespeare, Brady Timoney
翻　　譯	蘇瑞琴
編　　輯	Gina Wang
校　　對	陳慧莉
內文排版	劉秋筑
封面設計	林書玉
製程管理	洪巧玲
出 版 者	寂天文化事業股份有限公司
電　　話	+886-(0)2-2365-9739
傳　　真	+886-(0)2-2365-9835
網　　址	www.icosmos.com.tw
讀者服務	onlineservice@icosmos.com.tw
出版日期	2016 年 8 月 初版一刷

郵撥帳號 1998620-0 寂天文化事業股份有限公司
劃撥金額 600（含）元以上者，郵資免費。
訂購金額 600 元以下者，加收 65 元運費。
〔若有破損，請寄回更換，謝謝〕

國家圖書館出版品預行編目 (CIP) 資料

永恆的莎士比亞改寫劇本 .4 : 馬克白 / William
Shakespeare, Brady Timoney 作 : 蘇瑞琴譯 .-- 初版 .--
[臺北市] : 寂天文化 , 2016.08
面 ; 公分
ISBN 978-986-318-488-1(平裝附光碟片)

873.43361　　　　　　　　　　　105014694

Contents

Introduction

In the year 1040, Macbeth and Banquo, two victorious generals, meet three mysterious witches on a heath in Scotland. The witches predict that Macbeth will one day be King of Scotland. They tell Banquo that his sons will also sit on the throne.

Urged on by his wife, Macbeth kills King Duncan and is declared king. Fearing the second part of the witches' prophecy, Macbeth has Banquo killed. When Duncan's son Malcolm raises an army to oppose Macbeth, Lady Macbeth, tormented by guilt, commits suicide. Macbeth is then killed by Macduff, and Malcolm is crowned king.

Cast of Characters

DUNCAN King of Scotland

MALCOLM and **DONALBAIN** His sons

MACBETH General in the king's army

BANQUO General in the king's army

LENNOX, ROSS, MACDUFF, ANGUS, CAITHNESS, MENTEITH
Noblemen of Scotland

FLEANCE Son of Banquo

SIWARD: Earl of Northumberland, General of the
English Forces

YOUNG SIWARD His son

SEYTON An officer attending on Macbeth

BOY Son to Macduff

An **ENGLISH DOCTOR,** a **SCOTTISH DOCTOR,** a **SOLDIER,**
a **PORTER,** an **OLD MAN**

LADY MACBETH

LADY MACDUFF Gentlewoman attending on Lady Macbeth

THREE WITCHES

LORDS, GENTLEMEN, OFFICERS, SOLDIERS, MURDERERS,
ATTENDANTS, and **MESSENGERS**

The **GHOST OF BANQUO** and **SEVERAL OTHER APPARITIONS**

ACT 1

Summary

蘇格蘭正在打仗,在戰場附近,有三位女巫在風暴中會面,他們打算在日落前與蘇格蘭將領馬克白相見。同時,一位士兵向鄧肯國王稟報戰況,他報告馬克白在戰場上的英勇表現。

為了獎勵馬克白的表現,鄧肯封他為考德領主。女巫當晚與馬克白相遇時,即用此頭銜稱呼他,並告訴他驚人的預言,說他很快將成為國王。女巫們也告訴另一位將領班珂,說他的兒孫們將成為國王。隨後,鄧肯國王、他的兒子馬爾康和道南班、班珂及其他領主,前往馬克白的城堡因佛尼斯拜訪馬克白。馬克白夫人為了想成為皇后,慫恿丈夫殺了鄧肯國王。

Scene 1

(An open place. Thunder and lightning. **Three witches** enter.)

WITCH 1: When shall we three meet again?
In thunder, in lightning, or in rain?

WITCH 2: When the hurlyburly's done,
When the battle's lost and won.

WITCH 3: Before the setting of the sun.

WITCH 1: Where shall we meet?

WITCH 2: On the heath.

WITCH 3: There we will meet with Macbeth.

WITCH 1: Let's go home for now.

ALL: Fair is foul, and foul is fair—
Fly through the fog and filthy air.

(The **witches** vanish.)

──────Scene ❷ 🎧──────

(A camp near Forres. Alarms are heard offstage. **King Duncan**, **Malcolm**, **Donalbain**, and **Lennox** enter, with **attendants**. They meet a bleeding **soldier**.)

DUNCAN: What bloody man is that?
    From the way he looks, he can tell us
    How the battle is going.

MALCOLM: This is the man
    Who fought against my capture.
    (to the soldier): Hail, brave friend!
    How is the battle going?

SOLDIER: Macbeth's sword smoked as he
    Carved out his passage through the battle!
    Finally he faced the villain Macdonald.
    He didn't shake hands or say farewell.
    Instead, he cut him from belly to jaws
    And placed his head high on the castle
      walls.

DUNCAN: Oh, brave and worthy cousin!

SOLDIER: Then problems came from the east.
    Listen, King of Scotland, listen!
    When the rebels started to run, the
    Norwegian lord saw an advantage.

With fresh arms and new supplies of men,

He launched a new attack.

DUNCAN: Didn't this dismay

Our captains, Macbeth and Banquo?

SOLDIER: Yes—like a sparrow dismays an eagle

Or a hare dismays a lion!

They were, my king,

Like cannons with double charges!

For each stroke by the enemy,

They gave back two.

But I am faint. My wounds cry out!

DUNCAN: Your words and your wounds

Both tell of your honor.

(to the attendants): Go, get him doctors.

(**The soldier** exits, with **attendants**.)

(to Malcolm): Who comes here?

MALCOLM: The worthy thane of Ross.

(**Ross** enters.)

ROSS: God save the king!

DUNCAN: Where were you, worthy thane?

ROSS: In Fife, great king,

Where Norwegian flags fill the sky

And chill our people with fear.

The King of Norway himself, leading
   many men, began a battle.
He was helped by that most disloyal
   traitor, the Thane of Cawdor.
At last, Macbeth, dressed in armor,
Challenged him with greater strength.
Point for point, arm against arm,
Macbeth wore him down. In the end,
The victory fell on us.

DUNCAN: Great happiness!

ROSS: Now, Sweno, Norway's king,
   Wants to surrender.
   We forbade him to bury his men
   Until he paid us $10,000.

DUNCAN: Never again shall the
   Thane of Cawdor betray us!
   Go see to his instant death,
   And greet Macbeth with his former title.

ROSS: I'll see it done.

DUNCAN: What he has lost, noble Macbeth has
   won.

(**All** exit.)

Scene ❸ 🎧⑤

(A heath near Forres. Thunder. The **three witches** enter. A drum is heard offstage.)

WITCH 1: A drum, a drum!

Macbeth does come.

ALL: The weird sisters, hand in hand,

Travelers over sea and land,

Thus do go about, about.

Three times to yours, three times to mine,

And three times again, to make up nine.

That's it! The charm's wound up.

(**Macbeth** and **Banquo** enter.)

MACBETH: So foul and fair a day I have not

seen.

BANQUO: How far is it to Forres?

(He sees the witches.) What are these

creatures, so withered

And so wild in their clothing?

They do not look like inhabitants

Of the earth, and yet they are on it.

MACBETH: Speak, if you can. What are you?

WITCH 1: Hail, Macbeth, Thane of Glamis!

WITCH 2: Hail, Macbeth, Thane of Cawdor!

WITCH 3: Hail, Macbeth, who shall be king
hereafter!

BANQUO: Why do you draw back, Macbeth?
Why fear what sounds so fair?
(to the witches): In the name of truth,
Are you fantasies, or are you indeed
What you seem to be? You greet
My noble partner with fair predictions
About his future. You say he will have
Noble possessions and royal rank.
Why do you not speak to me?
If you can look into the seeds of time,
And say which grain will grow,
And which will not,
Speak then to me, who neither begs nor
fears your favors nor your hate.

WITCH 1: Hail!

WITCH 2: Hail!

WITCH 3: Hail!

WITCH 1: Lesser than Macbeth, and greater.

WITCH 2: Not so happy, yet much happier.

WITCH 3: Your sons and grandsons shall
Be kings, though you will not.
So all hail, Macbeth and Banquo!

WITCH 1: Banquo and Macbeth, all hail!

MACBETH: Tell me more. Since my father's
death,
I have been Thane of Glamis.
But how can I be Thane of Cawdor, too?
The Thane of Cawdor is still alive,
A well-to-do gentleman. And to be king
Is no more possible than to be
Thane of Cawdor. Say from where
You got this strange information.

And why have you stopped us on this
   godforsaken heath
With such greetings and prophecies?
Speak, I say!

(**Witches** vanish.)

BANQUO: Earth has bubbles, as water does,
   And these must be bubbles, too.
   Look! They have vanished!

MACBETH: Into the air,
   What seemed real has melted
   As breath into the wind.
   I wish they had stayed!

BANQUO: Were they really here?
   Or has some food we've eaten
   Taken our reason prisoner?

MACBETH: Your children shall be kings.

BANQUO: *You* shall be king!

MACBETH: And Thane of Cawdor, too.
   Isn't that what they said?

BANQUO: Yes. They used those very words.

(hearing a sound) Who's there?

(**Ross** and **Angus** enter.)

ROSS: The king has happily received

The news of your success, Macbeth!

He was astonished

When he heard of your brave deeds

In the battle against the rebels.

All reports proclaimed your praises

In his kingdom's great defense.

The king is very pleased to hear

Of your fearlessness during battle.

ANGUS: As advance payment

Toward an even greater honor, the king

Told me to call you Thane of Cawdor.

So I say, hail, most worthy thane!

The title is yours.

BANQUO: Those witches told the truth?

MACBETH: But the Thane of Cawdor lives!

Why do you dress me in borrowed robes?

ANGUS: He who was the thane still lives.

But he deserves to lose his life.

He might have actually fought for

Norway.

Or he might have helped the King of

Norway in hidden ways.

Perhaps he did both of these things
To work for the ruin of his own country.
I do not know exactly how he did it.
But the charges have been proven,
And he has confessed to treason.
The death sentence has been pronounced.

MACBETH *(aside)*: Thane of Glamis, and now
Thane of Cawdor, too!
And the greatest title is yet to come!
(to Banquo): Do you not hope your children
Shall be kings? After all, those who told me
That I would be the Thane of Cawdor
Promised no less to them.

BANQUO: If we trusted those promises fully,
You might be king as well.
But it is strange. Often, to bring harm to us,
The devil tells us small truths,
Winning us over with small things,
Only to betray us in important things.
(to Ross and Angus): Cousins, a word with
you, please.

MACBETH *(aside)*: Two of their predictions
Have come true! They seem like happy hints

To the greater prophecy that I will be king.

(to Ross and Angus): I thank you, gentlemen.

(aside): This supernatural prophecy

Might be evil or good. If evil,

Why has it given me evidence of success,

By starting with a truth? For it is true

That I am Thane of Cawdor.

If good, why are horrid thoughts

Making my heart knock at my ribs?

Imagined horrors are worse than real fears.

My thoughts about murdering the king

Shake me until I feel smothered.

Yet nothing else seems real to me.

BANQUO *(to Ross and Angus)*: Look at Macbeth.

He seems to be in a trance.

MACBETH *(aside)*: If my fate is to be king,

Then fate may crown me—

Even if I do nothing.

BANQUO *(to Ross and Angus)*: New honors come

upon Macbeth.

Like new clothes, they do not fit well

Until they've been used for a while.

MACBETH *(aside)*: Come what may,
Time and the hour runs through the
roughest day.

BANQUO: Worthy Macbeth, we're waiting.

MACBETH: Please forgive me.
My thoughts were wandering.
Let us go to meet the king.
(to Banquo): Think about what has happened.
Later, after we've considered things,
Let us speak freely about it.

BANQUO: Very gladly.

MACBETH: Until then, enough! Come, friends.

(**All** exit.)

Scene 4 6

(Forres. The palace. **King Duncan**, **Malcolm**, **Donalbain**, **Lennox**, and **attendants** enter.)

DUNCAN: Has the Thane of Cawdor been
  executed?
Have the officers returned yet?

MACBETH: Not yet, my lord. But I have
Spoken with one who saw Cawdor die.
After confessing his treasons,
He begged your highness's pardon.
Nothing in his life
Was as honorable as his leaving it.
He died as one who had rehearsed
Throwing away the dearest thing he
  owned
As if it were a careless trifle.

DUNCAN: Alas! There's no way
To read a man's mind in his face!
He was a gentleman in whom I placed
An absolute trust.

(**Macbeth**, **Banquo**, **Ross**, and **Angus** enter.)

(to Macbeth): Oh, most worthy cousin!
I owe you more than I can ever pay.

MACBETH: Serving you loyally
Is payment in itself. Your highness's role
Is to receive our services. Our duties
Are to do what we can to keep you safe.

DUNCAN: I have only begun to honor you.
Now I will work to see you prosper.
You, noble Banquo, you have deserved
No less. Let me embrace you
And hold you to my heart.

BANQUO: It is an honor to serve you, my lord.

DUNCAN: Sons, kinsmen, thanes,
And all you who are near to me, know this:
I appoint my eldest son, Malcolm,
  as my successor. From now on,
He will be called the Prince of
  Cumberland.
He is not the only one who will be honored.
Signs of nobility, like stars, shall shine
On all those who merit them.
Let us now go to Inverness
To visit Macbeth's castle.

MACBETH: I'll go on ahead and tell my wife
The joyful news of your approach.
(bowing) I humbly take my leave.

DUNCAN: My worthy Thane of Cawdor!

MACBETH *(aside)*: The Prince of Cumberland!
That is an obstacle,
On which I must fall down, or leap over—
For it lies in my way. Stars, hide your fires!
Let no light see my black and deep desires.

(**Macbeth** exits.)

DUNCAN: True, worthy Banquo!
I am fed on Macbeth's praises.
They are a banquet to me. Let us follow
Him who prospers to bid us welcome.
He is a kinsman without equal!

(**All** exit.)

Scene 5

(Inverness, Macbeth's castle. **Lady Macbeth** enters, carrying a letter.)

LADY MACBETH *(reading the letter)*: "The three witches proved they can predict the future. After they vanished into the air, some messengers came from the king. They called me 'Thane of Cawdor'—the same title the weird sisters called me! The witches had also said, 'All hail, Macbeth, who shall be king hereafter!' I thought it good to tell you of this, my dearest partner in greatness. Lose no time in rejoicing over the greatness that is promised! Keep this to yourself, and farewell."

(commenting on the letter): You were already Thane of Glamis, and now Thane of Cawdor.
You shall also be what you were promised.
Yet I do fear your nature.
It is too full of the milk of human kindness

To go the fastest way. You yearn to be great.

You have ambition. But your nature lacks

   the necessary ruthlessness.

What you deeply desire

You would attain through honest means.

You would not do anything dishonest

To get it. You need someone

To say, "You must do this, if you want that."

Hurry home, so I may pour my spirit

Into your ear! Let me push you,

With the strength of my own voice,

To overcome all that stands between you

And the golden crown.

Fate and the supernatural have already

Destined you for greatness.

(A **servant** enters.)

LADY MACBETH: What is your news?

SERVANT: The king comes here tonight.

LADY MACBETH: You are mad to say it!

   Isn't my husband with him? If it were so,

   He would have told me to prepare for it.

SERVANT: May it please you, it is true.
  Our thane is coming. The messenger
  Who brought the news was so weary
  From running, he had only enough
  Breath to deliver the message.

LADY MACBETH: Take care of him.

He brings great news.

(**Servant** exits.)

  The raven himself is hoarse
  From croaking the news of Duncan's fatal
    entrance.

LADY MACBETH

Come, you spirits,

Fill me, from head to toe, full

Of the worst cruelty! Make my blood thick.

Kill any feelings of remorse and sorrow

So that no tender female feelings

May shake my evil purpose.

Come, thick night!

Wrap yourself in the darkest smoke of hell

So my keen knife will not see

The wound it makes, nor will heaven

Peep through the blanket of the dark

To cry, "Stop, stop!"

(**Macbeth** enters.)

Great Glamis! Worthy Cawdor!

Greater than both, in the near future!

Your letter has carried me beyond

The ignorant present! I can feel

The future in this very instant!

MACBETH: My dearest love,

Duncan arrives tonight.

LADY MACBETH: And when does he leave?

MACBETH: Tomorrow, or so he plans.

LADY MACBETH: Oh, never
Shall he see the sun again!
Your face, my thane, is like a book
Where anyone can read strange things.
To fool the time, look like the time.
Show welcome in your eye,
Your hand, your words.
Look like the innocent flower
But be the serpent under it.
He who is coming must be provided for.
You shall put this night's great business
In my hands. I will take care of
    everything!
Then all our nights and days to come
Will be spent as king and queen.

MACBETH: We will speak further.

LADY MACBETH: Just remain calm.
Do nothing that looks suspicious.
Leave all the rest to me.

(**Both** exit.)

Scene **6** 🎧

(Before Macbeth's castle. **King Duncan**, **Malcolm**, **Donalbain**, **Banquo**, **Lennox**, **Macduff**, **Ross**, **Angus**, and **servants** enter.)

DUNCAN: This castle is in a pleasant place.

The air softly and sweetly appeals

To our gentle senses.

BANQUO *(pointing to a bird)***:** These birds often

Make their nests where the air is delicate.

(**Lady Macbeth** enters.)

DUNCAN: See, see, our honored hostess!

I thank you for the trouble you take

In preparing for our visit.

LADY MACBETH: Had we done twice as much,

And then twice that much again,

It would not equal the deep honor

Which your majesty brings to our house.

DUNCAN: Give me your hand, and show me

To my beloved host.

(**All** exit.)

Scene 7

(Within Macbeth's castle. **Macbeth** enters.)

MACBETH: If it must be done,
Then it's best done quickly.
If only the assassination could end it!
Followed by success, that would be fine.
But we still face judgment. This justice
Makes us think twice about such evil.
Duncan's here in double trust—
First, I am his kinsman and his subject.
This argues strongly against the deed.
Second, I am his host.
I should shut the door against his
   murderer,
Not bear the knife myself! Besides,
Duncan is a good man. His virtues
Plead like angels against his murder.
I have no good reason to do this,
Except my own ambition, which, like an
   eager rider, may jump over the horse,
And fall on the other side.

(**Lady Macbeth** enters.)

What news?

LADY MACBETH: He is almost finished supper.
Why have you left the room?

MACBETH: Has he asked for me?

LADY MACBETH: Don't you know he has?

MACBETH: We will go no further with the plan.
He has honored me, and I have earned
Golden opinions from all sorts of people.
I should wear these now while they are new
And not cast them aside so soon.

LADY MACBETH: What about your hopes
For the future? Have they been sleeping?
Are you afraid to be the same in your act
As you are in your desire? Would you
Live as a coward in your own eyes,
Saying "I dare not" rather than "I will"?
You are like the cat who wanted the fish
But was afraid to get its paws wet.

MACBETH: I beg you, be quiet!
I dare do all that a man may do.
Who dares to do more is not a man.

LADY MACBETH *(angrily):* What beast was it, then,
That made you talk about this plan to me?
When you dared to do it, you were a man.
To be more than you were,
You would be so much more the man.
Come now—you have sworn to do it!

MACBETH: What if we should fail?

LADY MACBETH: With enough courage, we'll not
fail. When Duncan is asleep,
I'll give his two guards wine and liquor.
They'll soon be asleep, too.

We'll kill the unguarded Duncan.

It will be easy

To blame his drunken guards, who

Shall bear the guilt of our great murder.

MACBETH: Yes! After we have marked with

Duncan's blood

Those two sleeping guards,

And used their very daggers for the crime,

Everyone will think they did it.

LADY MACBETH: Who could think otherwise—

Especially when we'll be crying the loudest

About his death?

MACBETH: Then it's settled.

Away, and fool the time with fairest show.

False face must hide what false heart does

know.

(**They** exit.)

ACT 2

Summary

當鄧肯國王熟睡時，馬克白用刀刺死了他，馬克白夫人將鄧肯的血沾抹在被下藥而昏睡的守衛身上。翌日清晨，麥德夫和雷諾克斯抵達因佛尼斯來求見國王。他們發現國王的屍首，馬克白因此殺了守衛，並將鄧肯之死怪罪於守衛身上。鄧肯的兒子雙雙逃離蘇格蘭——馬爾康逃到英格蘭而道南班逃至愛爾蘭。由於兩位王子皆潛逃出國，羅斯和麥德夫懷疑是王子買通守衛以謀殺父王。馬克白被加冕為蘇格蘭國王。

Scene ❶ 🎧

(The courtyard of Macbeth's castle. **Banquo**, **Fleance**, and a **servant** carrying a torch enter.)

BANQUO: What time is it, son?

SERVANT: After midnight, sir.

BANQUO: There is thriftiness in the heavens,
For the stars, like candles, are all out.
A heavy feeling lies on me like lead,
And yet I could not sleep. Merciful
Powers, hold back my cursed thoughts
That keep me from sleeping!
(hearing a noise): Who's there?

(**Macbeth** and a **servant** carrying a torch enter.)

MACBETH: A friend.

BANQUO: What, sir, not asleep yet?
The king's in bed. He was in a good mood
And sent great gifts to your officers.
He said your wife is a wonderful hostess,
And then he retired, very content.

MACBETH: Being unprepared for his visit,
I fear that we didn't do enough for him.

BANQUO: All was well. I dreamed last night
  Of the three weird sisters.
  For you, their first prediction has come true!

MACBETH: If you are loyal to me, honors
    shall be yours when the time comes.

BANQUO: I lose no honor in seeking to add to
    it. If I can keep my conscience
  Free while staying loyal, then, of course,
    I shall take your advice.

MACBETH: Sleep well, then!

BANQUO: Thank you, sir. The same to you!

(**Banquo, Fleance,** and their **servant** exit.)

MACBETH *(to his servant)*: Tell my wife to
  Strike the bell when my drink is ready.

(**Servant** exits.)

  Is this a dagger I seem to see before me,
  The handle toward my hand?
  Are you, fatal vision, able to be felt
  As well as seen? Or are you only
  A dagger of the mind, a false creation,
  Coming from my fevered brain?
  I can see you still, in a form as real

34

As this one, which now I draw.

(He draws out his own, real dagger.)

You show me the way I meant to go.

Are my eyes made fools by my

Other senses, or better than the rest?

I still see you. Your blade has bits of blood

That were not there before. You're not real.

This bloody business makes me see things!

Now half the world is slumbering.

Wicked dreams come to those who sleep.

Sure and firm earth, hear not my steps.

Do not notice which way they walk.

I fear your very stones tell where I am.

While I talk, Duncan still lives.

Words blow cold air on the heat of deeds.

(A bell rings.)

I go, and it is done. The bell invites me.

Hear it not, Duncan, for it calls from

Your grave in the cold ground.

(**Macbeth** exits. **Lady Macbeth** enters.)

LADY MACBETH: That which made them drunk

Has made me bold. What quenched

Their thirst has set me afire. Listen!
The owl shrieks, the fatal bellman
Which says the last good night.
Ah! I see the drunken guards
Mock their king with snores. I have drugged
Their drinks, so that death and nature
Fight over them, whether they live or die.

MACBETH *(offstage)*: What's going on?

LADY MACBETH *(to herself)*: Alas! They've
 awakened,

And it is not done yet. The attempt,
And not the deed, ruins us!
I put their daggers out in plain sight.
He could not miss them. If Duncan had
Not looked like my own father in his
   sleep, I would have done it myself.

(**Macbeth** enters again, covered with blood.)

LADY MACBETH: My husband!

MACBETH: I have done the deed.
   Did you not hear a noise?

LADY MACBETH: I heard the owl scream
   And the crickets cry.

MACBETH: One man laughed in his sleep.
   Another one cried, "Murder!"
   They seemed to wake each other up,
   But quickly went back to sleep.

LADY MACBETH: Two guests are sleeping in a
   room near Duncan's.

MACBETH: One cried, "God bless us!"
   The other said, "Amen."
   I feared that they had seen me

With these bloody hands.
Hearing their fear, I could not say, "Amen"
When they said, "God bless us!"

LADY MACBETH: Your thoughts are too deep.

MACBETH: But why could I not say, "Amen"?
I had most need of blessing,
And "Amen" stuck in my throat.

LADY MACBETH: We must not dwell on these
deeds, or we will go mad.

MACBETH: I heard a voice cry, "Sleep no more!
Macbeth does murder sleep!"
Only the innocent sleep—sleep that
Knits up the raveled sleave of care,
The death of each day's worries,
Medicine for hurt minds,
The greatest nourisher in life's feast.

LADY MACBETH: What do you mean?

MACBETH: Still it cried, "Sleep no more!"
To all the house. "Glamis has murdered sleep,
And therefore Cawdor shall sleep no more.
Macbeth shall sleep no more!"

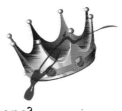

LADY MACBETH: Who cried this out, worthy thane?
You are wasting your noble strength
Thinking such foolish thoughts. Go wash
This filthy evidence from your hands.
Why did you bring these daggers with you?
They must lie there. Go, take them back!
Smear the sleeping guards with blood!

MACBETH: I can't go back. I'm afraid to look
upon what I have done!

LADY MACBETH: Coward! I'll take the daggers.
The sleeping and the dead are but pictures
Of each other. Only a child would fear them!
I'll paint the guards' faces with his blood
To make them look guilty.

(**She** exits. A knocking is heard.)

MACBETH: What is that knocking?
Why does every noise frighten me?
What hands are these?
Will all the ocean wash away this blood?
My hands could make the green seas red!

(**Lady Macbeth** enters again.)

LADY MACBETH: My hands are of your color,
But I am ashamed to wear a heart so white.

(More knocking.)

LADY MACBETH: I hear knocking at the south entry.
Let's go to our chamber and wash our hands.
How easy it is then!

(More knocking.)

Listen! More knocking.
Get on your nightclothes. We must look
As if we've been sleeping. Don't be lost
So poorly in your thoughts.

MACBETH: I'd rather be lost in thought than
Have to look at my deed.

(More knocking.)

Wake Duncan with your knocking! I wish
you could!

(**Both** exit. A **porter** enters. More knocking.)

PORTER: Who's knocking? I'm coming!

(He opens the gate. **Macduff and Lennox** enter.)

MACDUFF: Is your master awake? Oh, I see that
Our knocking waked him. Here he comes.

(**Macbeth** enters, wearing nightclothes.)

LENNOX: Good morning, noble sir!

MACBETH: Good morning, both of you!

MACDUFF: Is the king awake, worthy thane?

MACBETH: Not yet, I think.

MACDUFF: He told me to call on him early.
I've almost missed the time he requested.

MACBETH: There's the door to his chamber.

(**Macduff** exits.)

LENNOX: Is the king leaving today?

MACBETH: Yes. At least, that's what he said.

LENNOX: The night has been wild. Where we
Were sleeping, our chimneys blew down.
And they say there was wailing heard,
Strange screams of death, and
Terrible predictions of fire and confusion.
The owl shrieked all night.
Some say the feverish earth was shaking!

MACBETH: It was a rough night.

LENNOX: I cannot remember another like it.

(**Macduff** enters again.)

MACDUFF *(upset)*: Oh, horror, horror, horror!
  Neither tongue nor heart
  Can imagine or name it!

MACBETH AND LENNOX: What's the matter?

MACDUFF: Confusion has made its masterpiece!
  A most unholy murder has broken open
  The lord's holy temple, and stolen from it
  The life of the building.

MACBETH: What is it you say—the life?

LENNOX: Do you mean his majesty?

MACDUFF: Approach his room,
  And destroy your sight by looking.
  Do not ask me to speak!
  See, and then speak yourselves.

(**Macbeth** and **Lennox** exit.)

  Awake, awake!
  Ring the alarm bell! Murder and treason!
  Banquo and Donalbain! Malcolm! Awake!
  Shake off this gentle sleep, death's copy,
  And look on death itself! Up, up, and see
  The sight of the great doom!

Malcolm! Banquo!

Rise up to see this horror!

(Alarm bell rings. **Lady Macbeth** enters again.)

LADY MACBETH: What's all this?

Why such a terrible noise

To wake the sleepers of this house? Speak!

MACDUFF: Oh, gentle lady,

It is not for you to hear my words.

To repeat them in a woman's ear

Would murder her as the words were said.

(**Banquo** enters again.)

> Oh, Banquo, Banquo!
> Our royal master has been murdered!

LADY MACBETH: Woe, alas! In our house?

BANQUO: It would be too cruel anywhere.

> Dear Macduff, I beg you, say it is not so.

(**Macbeth**, **Lennox**, and **Ross** enter.)

MACBETH: If only I had died an hour ago,

> I would have lived a blessed time.
> Now there's nothing serious in life.
> All is but toys. Honor and grace are dead.
> The wine of life has been poured.
> Only the dregs are left.

(**Malcolm** and **Donalbain** enter.)

DONALBAIN: What is wrong?

MACBETH: You are—and you do not know it.

> The spring, the fountain of your blood,
> Is stopped. The very source of it is stopped.

MACDUFF: Your royal father is murdered.

MALCOLM: Oh, no! By whom?

LENNOX: It seems that his own guards did it.

Their hands and faces were covered in blood.

So were their daggers, which we found,

Unwiped, on their pillows.

No man's life was to be trusted with them.

MACBETH: Even so, I am sorry for the fury

That made me kill them.

MACDUFF: Why did you do it, then?

MACBETH: Who can be wise and confused,

Calm and furious, loyal and neutral,

All at once? No man. My love for Duncan

Outran my reason. Here lay our king,

His silver skin laced with his golden blood.

There were the murderers, covered in

Duncan's blood, their daggers

Smeared with gore! Anyone who

Had a heart to love, and in that heart

Courage to make that love known,

Would have done the same.

LADY MACBETH *(fainting)*: Help me!

MACDUFF: Look after the lady.

MALCOLM *(aside to Donalbain)*: Why do we
　　Hold our tongues, while everyone else
　　Talks about this subject so important to us?

DONALBAIN *(aside to Malcolm)*: We are not safe.
　　Our fate might be hiding
　　In some secret place, ready to rush out
　　And seize us. Let's get away.
　　We can cry over our father's death later.

BANQUO: Look after the lady.

(**Lady Macbeth** is carried out.)

　　Let's all go and get dressed.
　　Then let us meet here later to talk about
　　This most bloody piece of work
　　And try to learn more about it.
　　Fears and doubts shake us.
　　In the great hand of God I stand,
　　And from there, I will fight
　　Against the unknown forces of
　　Treason and evil.

MACDUFF: And so will I.

ALL: And so will we all.

MACBETH: Let's put on our armor,
And meet together in the hall.

(**All** but **Malcolm** and **Donalbain** exit.)

MALCOLM: What will you do?
Let's not meet with the others.
Showing an unfelt sorrow is something
That false men do easily. I will go to
England.

DONALBAIN: And I'll go to Ireland.
We'll be safer if we are separated.
Where we are now, there are daggers
In men's smiles. Our closest relations
Are the most likely to kill us.

MALCOLM: The murderous arrow
That's been shot has not yet landed.
Our safest course is to avoid the aim.
Let us not say goodbye to anyone,
But secretly steal away. There's no honor
Where there's no mercy left.

(**Malcolm** and **Donalbain** exit.)

——Scene **2** ——

(Outside Macbeth's castle. **Ross** and **Macduff** enter.)

ROSS: Is it known who did this bloody deed?

MACDUFF: The guards that Macbeth killed.

ROSS: But what was their motive?

MACDUFF: They were hired by someone.
Malcolm and Donalbain, the king's sons,
Have run away. This makes them look
guilty to the thanes.

ROSS: An act against nature! Why would
They want to kill their own father?
Now it is most likely that the crown will
Pass on to Macbeth.

MACDUFF: He has already been named king.
He has gone to Scone to be crowned.

ROSS: Where is Duncan's body?

MACDUFF: It's been carried to Scone,
To the sacred tomb of Scottish kings.

ROSS: Will you go to Scone?

MACDUFF: No, cousin. I'll go home, to Fife.

ROSS: Well, I'll go to Scone.

MACDUFF: May you see things well-done there
Farewell!

ROSS: And farewell to you.

(**Ross** and **Macduff** exit.)

ACT3

Summary

當班珂仔細思考女巫的話語，他發現所有關於馬克白的預言皆已成真，他記起女巫話中關於自己子嗣的命運，並對他們的未來寄予厚望。

馬克白與殺手計畫謀殺班珂和佛良斯，當班珂慘遭殺害時，佛良斯逃跑了。當晚，馬克白和其夫人，同時也是新國王與皇后，設宴款待賓客。當賓客入座後，馬克白看見班珂的鬼魂。他與鬼魂對話，同時也明顯暴露他與班珂謀殺案的牽連。馬克白夫人要求賓客離開，謊稱丈夫身體不適。麥德夫懷疑馬克白行兇，遂前往英格蘭，計畫得到愛德華國王的援助，出兵攻打馬克白。

Scene ❶ 🎧12

(Forres. A room in the palace. **Banquo** enters.)

BANQUO *(to himself)*: You have it now—

King, Cawdor, Glamis—

All that the weird sisters promised.

If they told the truth about you,

Perhaps they told the truth about me

As well. If so, I have strong hopes.

But hush, no more.

(Trumpets sound. **Macbeth** enters as king, followed by
Lady Macbeth as queen, **Lennox**, **Ross**, **lords**,
ladies, and **attendants**.)

MACBETH: A banquet is being held tonight, sir,

And I want you to be there.

BANQUO: Your wish is my command, highness.

MACBETH: Are you going riding this afternoon?

BANQUO: Yes, my good lord.

MACBETH: Will you be riding far?

BANQUO: As far, my lord, as will fill up

The time between now and supper.

MACBETH: Do not fail to come to the feast.

BANQUO: My lord, I will not.

MACBETH: We hear that our bloody cousins,
Malcolm and Donalbain, have gone to
England and to Ireland. They have not
Confessed to killing their father.
Instead, they fill their hearers' ears
With wild stories about his death.
But we'll talk about that tomorrow.
Farewell, until you return at night.
Is Fleance going with you?

BANQUO: Yes, my good lord.

(**Banquo** exits. **Macbeth** speaks to the others.)

MACBETH: You may do whatever you like
Until seven tonight. To make the company
Even sweeter then, we will stay alone this
afternoon. God be with you.

(**All** exit but **Macbeth** and a **servant**.)

MACBETH *(to the servant)*: We sent for some
men. Are they here yet?

SERVANT: Yes, my lord. They are at the gate.

MACBETH: Bring them before us.

(**Servant** exits.)

MACBETH: To be king is nothing,

Unless one's position is safe.

Our fears about Banquo run deep.

He threatens my greatness.

When the weird sisters called me king,

They called him father to a line of kings.

Upon my head they placed a fruitless

  crown, to be taken from me one day

By no son of mine.

If the prophecies are true,

I have murdered the gracious Duncan

Just to make Banquo's sons kings!

Rather than that, let fate come to

The battle as my champion.

(He hears a noise.) Who's there?

(**Servant** enters again, with **two murderers**.)

Go to the door until we call.

(**Servant** exits.)

Was it not yesterday we spoke together?

MURDERER 1: It was, your highness.

MACBETH: Well, then, have you considered

What I said? Do you understand

That it was Banquo who was responsible
For your bad fortune in the past, and not
My innocent self, as you had thought?

MURDERER 1: You made it known to us.

MACBETH: Can you forgive? Are you so
Good that you can pray for him
When his heavy hand has ruined you
And made beggars of your own children?

MURDERER 1: We are men, my lord.

MACBETH: Yes, in the list of species,
You are described as men,
Just as hounds, greyhounds, mongrels,
Spaniels, curs, waterdogs, and wolves are
All called by the name of dogs.
The best kind of list tells the difference
Between the swift, the slow, the wild,
The housedog, the hunter. Each one has
A special gift granted by nature.
And so it is with men.
Do you rate yourselves above
The worst rank of men? Say so,
And I will give you a special assignment

Which will take your enemy off the list
And bring you closer to my affection.
For I wear my health sickly while he lives,
But with his death, my life will be perfect.

MURDERER 2: My lord, I am one who is
So angry at the evil blows of the world
That I am reckless about what I do
To spite the world.

MURDERER 1: And I am another—so weary
With disasters, tugged by bad luck,
That I would bet my life on any chance
To mend it or be rid of it.

MACBETH: You know Banquo was your enemy.

BOTH MURDERERS: True, my lord.

MACBETH: He is my enemy, too.
Every minute of his being feels like a
Knife thrust to my heart. Though I could
Sweep him from sight with my power,
I must not do so. Certain friends that are
Both his and mine would mourn his fall,
And I need their loyalty.
This is why I ask your help. Do this—
But let no suspicion fall on me!

MURDERER 2: My lord, we shall do as you ask.

MACBETH: It must be done tonight.
And it must be done away from the palace.
Remember that I must not be suspected.
Do not botch this work!
Fleance, Banquo's son, will be with him.
His death is no less important to me
Than his father's. He must face the fate
Of that dark hour. Wait outside the gate.
I'll come to you soon with more
 instructions.

(**Murderers** exit.)

It is arranged. Banquo, your soul's flight,
If it is to heaven, must find it out tonight.

(**Macbeth** exits.)

Scene **2**

(**Lady Macbeth** and a **servant** enter a room in the palace.)

LADY MACBETH: Tell the king to come to me.

SERVANT: Madam, I will.

(**Servant** exits.)

LADY MACBETH: Nothing is ours, all is spent,

When we have our desire but are not content.

(**Macbeth** enters.)

My lord! Why look so sad?

Things that cannot be changed

Should be forgotten. What's done is done.

MACBETH: We have cut the snake, not killed it.

She'll heal herself, and then we will

Be in great danger. It would be better

To be with the peaceful dead,

Than to suffer this torture of the mind.

Duncan is in his grave.

After life's fitful fever, he sleeps well.

Treason has done his worst.

Nothing can touch him further.

LADY MACBETH: Come on, my gentle lord.
Sleek over your rugged looks.
Be bright and happy with our guests
tonight.

MACBETH: I shall, my love.
And so, I hope, shall you.
Let your attention be given to Banquo.
Show him honor, both with your eyes
And with your words. For a while yet,
We are unsafe. We must make our faces
Masks to our hearts, disguising them.

LADY MACBETH: You must stop this.

MACBETH: Oh, full of scorpions is my mind,
Dear wife! Banquo and Fleance live.

LADY MACBETH: But they won't live forever.

MACBETH: That's comforting, so be joyful.
Before the bat has flown from its cave
Into the darkness of the night,
A dreadful deed shall be done.

LADY MACBETH: What's to be done?

MACBETH: Be innocent of the knowledge
Until you applaud the deed. Come, night!

Blindfold the tender eye of pitiful day.
With your bloody and invisible hand
Cancel and tear to pieces that great bond
That keeps me pale! Light thickens,
And the crow makes wing to the woods.
The good day begins to droop and drowse,
While night's black agents go to their prey.
You wonder at my words, but you'll see
How evil makes bad things even worse.
So, please, go with me.

(**Both** exit.)

Scene ❸ (14)

(A park near the palace. **Three murderers** enter.)

MURDERER 1: Who told you to join us?

MURDERER 3: Macbeth.

MURDERER 2 *(to murderer 1)***:** We have

No reason to mistrust him.

He gave us our orders.

MURDERER 1: Then stand with us.

The west still glimmers with streaks of day.

The late traveler is hurrying along

To reach an inn before dark.

Soon, those we wait for will approach.

MURDERER 3: Listen! I hear horses.

BANQUO *(offstage)***:** Give us a light there!

MURDERER 2: That must be Banquo.

The rest of the dinner guests

Are already in the court.

MURDERER 1: The groom is taking the horses

To the stable. Banquo and Fleance

Will walk to the palace gate.

MURDERER 2: I see a light! A light!

MURDERER 3: They're almost here! Get ready!

(**Banquo** and **Fleance** enter. **Fleance** carries a torch.)

BANQUO: It looks like rain tonight.

MURDERER 1: Let it pour!

(**Murderer 1** strikes out the light. The others attack **Banquo**.)

BANQUO: Oh, treachery! Run, good Fleance!

　　Run, run, run! Avenge me later! Farewell!

(**Banquo** dies. **Fleance** escapes.)

MURDERER 3: Who struck out the light?

MURDERER 1: Wasn't that the best way?

MURDERER 3: There's only one down.

　　The son has fled.

MURDERER 2: We have failed

　　In the most important part of our job!

MURDERER 1: We must go and tell Macbeth.

(**All** exit.)

Scene 4

(The banquet room in the palace. **Macbeth**, **Lady Macbeth**, **Ross**, **Lennox**, **lords**, and **attendants** enter.)

MACBETH: Welcome! You know your own ranks.

Sit in your proper places.

LORDS: Thanks to your majesty.

MACBETH: I'll mingle with our guests,

And play the humble host.

Our hostess will welcome you

At the proper time.

LADY MACBETH: Please say it for me, sir.

Tell all our friends,

For my heart says they are welcome.

MACBETH *(to Lady Macbeth)*: See—our guests

Meet you with their hearts' thanks.

(to guests): Both sides of the table are even.

I will sit in the middle.

(**Murderer 1** enters and stands near the door.)

Enjoy yourselves. Soon we'll have a toast

To start off the meal.

(**Macbeth** walks toward the door as the guests talk. He whispers to **Murderer 1**.)

There's blood on your face.

MURDERER 1: It is Banquo's, then.

MACBETH: Better outside you than inside him.
Is he dead?

MURDERER 1: My lord, his throat is cut.
That I did for him.

MACBETH: You are the best of the cutthroats.
Who did the same for Fleance?
If you did it, you are surely the best.

MURDERER 1: Most royal sir, Fleance escaped.

MACBETH: Oh, no! That's terrible!
My life would have been perfect,
As broad and free as the air.
But now I am confined, bound in
By doubts and fears. But Banquo's dead?

MURDERER 1: Yes, my good lord.
Dead in a ditch he lies,
With twenty gashes on his head,
The least of which would have killed him.

MACBETH: My thanks for that.
    The grown serpent lies dead. The worm
    That has fled will soon have venom—
    But as yet he has no teeth. Go now.
    Tomorrow we'll talk again.

(**Murderer 1** exits.)

LADY MACBETH: My royal lord,
    You did not give the toast! It's no feast
    Without a ceremony. Mere eating is best
    Done at home. Away from home,
    Ceremony is the sauce to the meat.
    A feast is bare without it. Be a good host.
    Make your guests feel welcome.

MACBETH: Sweet reminder!
    Now, good health to all! Enjoy the feast.

LENNOX: May it please your highness to sit.

(The **ghost of Banquo**, visible only to **Macbeth**, enters
and sits in Macbeth's place. Macbeth does not see it yet.)

MACBETH: All the noblemen of our country
    Would be seated under one roof,
    If only Banquo were present. I hope
    It is thoughtlessness rather than some

Accident that has made him late.

ROSS: His absence, sir, breaks his promise.

Would it please your highness to be seated?

MACBETH: The table's full.

LENNOX: Here is an empty seat, sir.

MACBETH: Where?

LENNOX: Right here, my good lord.

(**Lennox** sees that **Macbeth** seems upset. **Macbeth** has just set eyes on **Banquo's ghost**.)

What's wrong, your highness?

MACBETH: Which of you has done this?

LORDS: What, my good lord?

MACBETH *(to ghost)*: You cannot say I did it!
  Do not shake your bloody hair at me.

ROSS: Gentlemen, rise. His highness is ill.

LADY MACBETH: Sit, worthy friends.
  My lord is often like this, and has been
  Since his youth. Please, stay seated.
  The fit is temporary. In a moment,
  He will again be well. If you stare,
  You will offend him and make it worse.

Eat, and pay no attention to him.

(aside, to Macbeth): Are you a man?

MACBETH: Yes, and a bold one, who dares
Look on that which might scare the devil.

LADY MACBETH *(aside to Macbeth)*: Nonsense!
What are you afraid of? Shame on you!
Why do you make such faces? In the end,
You're only looking at a stool.

MACBETH: No, see there? Behold! Look!
Can't you see it?

(*to the ghost*): Why, what do I care?

If you cannot nod, you cannot speak, either.

Do our graves send back those we bury?

Maybe we should feed our dead to the birds.

(**Ghost** disappears.)

ACT 3
SCENE
4

LADY MACBETH (*aside to Macbeth*): Shame!

MACBETH: As I am standing here, I saw him.

Blood has been shed before now.

Yes, and murders have been performed

That are too terrible to hear about.

In the past, when the brains were hit,

The man would die, and that would end it.

But now they rise again,

And push us from our stools.

This is much stranger than murder!

LADY MACBETH: My worthy lord,

Your noble friends are waiting for you.

MACBETH: Oh! I almost forgot.

Do not wonder at me, my worthy friends.

I have a strange illness, which is nothing

To those who know me.

Come, love and health to you all!

Give me some wine, a full glass.
I drink to the joy of the whole table, and to
Our dear friend Banquo, whom we miss.
We drink to all and to him!

LORDS: To the joy of all!

(The **ghost** enters again.)

MACBETH *(to the ghost):* Quit my sight!
Let the earth hide you! Your bones have
No marrow. Your blood is cold.
Those glaring eyes cannot see!

LADY MACBETH: Think of this, good lords,
As just a sad ailment. It's no more.
Don't let it spoil your pleasure.

MACBETH *(to the ghost):* What a man dares,
I dare. Approach like a rugged Russian bear,
An armored rhinoceros, or a wild tiger!
Take any shape but your own, and my nerves
Shall never tremble. Or be alive again, and
Dare me to a fight with your sword.
If I tremble at all, call me a little girl's doll.
Go away, horrible mocking shadow!

(The **ghost** disappears.)

68

Why, now it is gone.

I am myself again. Please, be seated, all.

LADY MACBETH: You've chased away the cheer

And ruined the whole evening

With your amazing disorder!

MACBETH: Can such things appear,

And overcome us like a summer's cloud,

Without our special wonder? You make me

A stranger to myself when I think

You can behold such sights,

And keep the natural ruby of your cheeks,

When mine are white with fear.

ROSS: What sights, my lord?

LADY MACBETH: Please, do not speak to him.

He grows worse and worse.

Questions enrage him. And so, good night.

Do not leave in the order of your ranks,

But all go at once.

LENNOX: Good night. May better health

Come to his majesty!

LADY MACBETH: A kind good night to all!

(**Lords** and **attendants** exit.)

MACBETH: The ghost wants revenge, I know.
Blood will be repaid in blood.
What time is it?

LADY MACBETH: Almost midnight.

MACBETH: What do you say to the fact that
Macduff did not come to the coronation
And ignored this banquet as well?

LADY MACBETH: Did he send a messenger?

MACBETH: No, he didn't.
But I will send one to him tomorrow.
I have at least one spy among the servants
At each nobleman's house,
So I know what Macduff has been saying.
Tomorrow I will visit the weird sisters,
For now I am determined to know,
By the worst methods, the worst news.
For my own good, all other matters
Must come second. I am standing so deep
In blood now that, if it were a river,
I would have to cross it. At this point,
It is easier to move on than to wade back.

I have strange ideas in my head,
And I must act upon them.

LADY MACBETH: You need some sleep.

MACBETH: Come, we'll sleep then.
My strange vision of the ghost
Is the fear of a beginner in evil.
We are yet but young in deed.

(**They** exit.)

Scene 5 🎧

(**Lennox** and **another lord** enter a room in the palace.)

LENNOX: Strange things have been happening.

The gracious Duncan visited Macbeth,

And soon was dead.

Then the brave Banquo, out walking late,

Was killed by his son Fleance, who fled—

   Or so Macbeth would have us believe.

Who cannot help thinking how monstrous

It was for Malcolm and Donalbain

To kill their gracious father? A terrible thing!

How it grieved Macbeth! Didn't he kill

The two guards in an angry rage? Anyone

Could see that they had been

Drinking too much and were sound asleep.

Wasn't that a noble act of Macbeth's?

Yes, and wise, too—for it would have

   angered

Any heart alive to hear the guards deny it.

I wonder what Macbeth would do if he had

Duncan's sons and Fleance locked up.

I'm sure they'd soon see the punishment for

Killing a father. But, enough about that!

I hear Macduff lives in disgrace, too,

For failing to come to the tyrant's feast.

Sir, can you tell me where Macduff is now?

LORD: Malcolm, Duncan's son,

From whom Macbeth stole the crown,

Is in England now, at King Edward's court.

Macduff has gone to England, too,

To help raise an army against Macbeth,

Who wants war with England.

If Malcolm and Macduff are successful,

We may again live in peace someday,

Without fear of bloody knives at banquets.

LENNOX: May a holy angel fly to the court

Of England to help Macduff.

May a swift blessing soon return

To our suffering country!

LORD: I'll send my prayers with him.

(**Both** exit.)

ACT 4

Summary

馬克白再度造訪三位女巫並探詢自己
未來的命運，她們給他看一系列的幻
象，並透過謎語的方式透露他的未來。

接著女巫消失，雷諾克斯抵達，他向馬克白報告麥德夫已逃
至英格蘭。馬克白對此消息甚感憤怒，命令殺手謀殺麥德
夫的妻子、兒女與所有在場的從僕。殺手抵達麥德夫的城堡
伐夫，殺了所有城堡內的人。

在英格蘭，馬爾康和麥德夫正在擬訂計畫，希望能恢復蘇格
蘭王國的和平，並談到英格蘭國王愛德華誓言出手相助。羅
斯之後捎來麥德夫妻小被謀殺的消息，使麥德夫備感震驚，
更痛下決心要推翻馬克白。

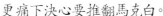

Scene ❶ 🎧17

(A dark cave with a cauldron boiling in the middle. Thunder sounds. The **three witches** enter.)

WITCH 1: Round about the cauldron go;

    Into the pot these things we'll throw.

ALL: Double, double, toil and trouble.

    Fire, burn, and cauldron, bubble.

WITCH 2: From the swamp came this snake.

    In the cauldron boil and bake.

    Eye of newt and toe of frog,

    Wool of bat and tongue of dog,

    For a charm of powerful trouble,

    Broth of evil, boil and bubble.

ALL: Double, double, toil and trouble,

    Fire, burn, and cauldron, bubble.

WITCH 3: Tooth of wolf, and dragon's scale,

    Witch's mummy, eye and nail,

    Add a little, then a lot,

    All these go into the pot.

ALL: Double, double, toil and trouble.

    Fire, burn, and cauldron, bubble.

ACT 4
SCENE 1

WITCH 2: Cool it with a baboon's blood,
Then the charm is firm and good.

WITCH 3: By the prickling in my thumbs,
Something wicked this way comes.
Open, locks, whoever knocks!
(**Macbeth** enters.)

MACBETH: You secret, midnight hags!
What is it you do?

ALL: A deed without a name.

MACBETH: I want to ask you some questions.

WITCH 1: Us or our masters?

MACBETH: Call them. Let me see them.

WITCH 1: Pour in sow's blood, that has eaten
    Her nine piglets. And some sweat
    Taken from a murderer's gallows.
    Throw these into the flame.

ALL: Come, high or low;
    To ourselves, yourself show!

(Thunder sounds. **Vision 1,** a head wearing armor, appears, rising out of the cauldron.)

VISION 1: Macbeth! Macbeth! Macbeth!
    Beware Macduff. Beware the thane
      of Fife.
    I go. I've said enough.

(**Vision 1** disappears into the cauldron.)

WITCH 1: He will not appear again.
    Here's another, more powerful than
      the first.

(Thunder sounds. **Vision 2,** a bloody child, appears, rising out of the cauldron.)

VISION 2: Be strong, bold, and firm.

Laugh to scorn the power of man, for

None of woman born shall harm Macbeth!

(**Vision 2** disappears into the cauldron.)

MACBETH: Then live, Macduff!

Why should I fear you? But,

Just to be sure, I'll make a deal with fate—

You shall not live, so I may put

All my pale-hearted fear to rest,

And sleep in spite of thunder.

(Thunder sounds. **Vision 3**, a crowned child, appears, holding a tree and rising out of the cauldron.)

MACBETH: What is this, rising like a king's son,

Wearing on his baby brow the crown

And signs of royalty?

ALL: Listen, but do not speak to it.

VISION 3: Be brave as a lion, and be proud.

Do not worry about your enemies.

Macbeth shall never be beaten until

Birnam Wood comes to Dunsinane Hill

And fights against him.

(**Vision 3** disappears into the cauldron.)

MACBETH: That will never be!

Who can force a forest to fight a war?
Sweet words, good! Rebel armies will
Not rise until the wood of Birnam rises.
Royal Macbeth shall live as long
As nature intended. Yet my heart throbs
To know one thing: Tell me if Banquo's sons
Shall ever reign in this kingdom.

ALL: Seek to know no more.

MACBETH: I must know! Deny me this,
And an eternal curse fall on you!
  Tell me—

ALL: Show his eyes, and grieve his heart.
Come like shadows, then depart!

(A show of **eight kings** and **Banquo**, the last, rises
from the cauldron holding a mirror.)

MACBETH *(speaking to each king in turn)*:
You are too much like the spirit of Banquo!
Go back down! Your crown burns my eyes!
And your hair is golden, like the first one.
A third is like the others. Filthy hags!
Why do you show me this? A fourth!
What, will the line never end?
Another yet! A seventh! I'll see no more!

And yet the eighth appears, with a mirror
That shows me many more. Horrible sight!
Now I see, it is true. They will all be kings!
The blood-spattered Banquo smiles at me,
And points at them, as if to say they are his.
What! Is this so?

WITCH 1: Yes, sir, all this is so. But why
Does Macbeth stand here so amazed?
Come, sisters, let's take our leave.
I'll charm the air to give a sound,
While you perform your dances round,
So this great king may kindly say,
We answered his questions on this day.

(Music. The **witches** dance and then vanish.)

MACBETH: Where are they? Gone?
Let this evil hour be accursed!
I hear someone coming.
Come in, whoever is out there!

(**Lennox** enters.)

LENNOX: What is your grace's will?

MACBETH: Did you see the weird sisters?

LENNOX: No, my lord.

MACBETH: Did they not pass by you?

LENNOX: No, indeed, my lord.

MACBETH: I heard the galloping of a horse.
Who was it that came by?

LENNOX: A few of us came to tell you
That Macduff has fled to England.

MACBETH: Fled to England!

LENNOX: Yes, my good lord.

MACBETH *(aside)*: If I hadn't come here,
I might have had time to stop Macduff.
From now on, as soon as I think about
Doing something, I will do it.
I will surprise Macduff's castle and
Give the edge of the sword to his wife,
His babes, and all unlucky relatives who
Might happen to be there.
I will not boast about it like a fool.
This deed I'll do before my anger cools.
(to Lennox): Where are these gentlemen?
Come, bring me where they are.

(**All** exit.)

Scene **2** 🎧18

(Fife. A room in Macduff's castle. **Lady Macduff**, **her son**, and **Ross** enter.)

LADY MACDUFF: What had he done,
　To make him leave Scotland?

ROSS: You must have patience, madam.

LADY MACDUFF: He had none.
　His flight was madness. His action
　Makes him look like a traitor.

ROSS: You do not know whether he left
　Out of wisdom or of fear.

LADY MACDUFF: Wisdom! To leave his wife,
　To leave his babes, his castle, and his title,
　In a place from which he himself does fly?
　He loves us not. He lacks natural feelings.
　Even the wren, the smallest of birds,
　Will fight the owl to protect her babies.
　He is all fear and no love, running away
　Against all reason.

ROSS: My dear cousin, I beg you, calm down.

Your husband is noble, wise, and careful.

He best knows the problems of the day.

I dare not speak further.

But the times are cruel when we are accused

Of being traitors without knowing why!

We float upon a wild and violent sea,

Moving each way the waves take us.

I must leave, but I'll soon return.

Blessings on you, my pretty cousin!

(**Ross** exits.)

LADY MACDUFF: My son, your father's dead.

What will you do now? How will you live?

SON: As birds do, Mother.

LADY MACDUFF: What, on worms and flies?

SON: No, with whatever I can get, as they do.

LADY MACDUFF: Poor bird! Wouldn't you fear

The traps, the hunter, or the snares?

SON: Why should I, Mother?

Poor birds are not hunted.

My father is not dead, though you say so.

LADY MACDUFF: Yes, he is dead.

What will you do for a father?

SON: No, what will you do for a husband?

LADY MACDUFF: I can buy 20 at any market.

SON: Then you'll buy them to sell again.

LADY MACDUFF: You speak with such wit!

SON: Was my father a traitor, Mother?

LADY MACDUFF: Yes, he was.

SON: What is a traitor?

LADY MACDUFF: One who swears and lies.

SON: And do all traitors do so?

LADY MACDUFF: Everyone that does so
Is a traitor, and must be hanged.

SON: Must all who swear and lie be hanged?

LADY MACDUFF: Every one.

SON: Who must hang them?

LADY MACDUFF: Why, the honest men.

SON: Then the liars and swearers are fools,
For there are enough of them
To beat the honest men and hang them all.

LADY MACDUFF: God help you, poor monkey!
But what will you do for a father?

SON: If he were dead, you'd weep for him.

If you don't weep for him, it's a good sign

That I will quickly have a new father.

LADY MACDUFF: How you talk!

(A **messenger** enters.)

MESSENGER: Bless you, fair lady! You don't

Know me, but I know who you are.

You must get away from here.

Run, with your little ones!

There are those who mean to do you harm.

Heaven help you! I dare stay here no longer.

(**Messenger** exits.)

LADY MACDUFF: Where should I go?

I have done no harm. But I remember now

I am in this earthly world. To do harm is

Often praiseworthy. To do good can be

Dangerous folly. Why, then, alas,

Do I put up that womanly defense,

To say I have done no harm?

(**Murderers** enter.)

Who are you?

MURDERER 1: Where is your husband?

LADY MACDUFF: I hope he is in no place so bad
Where such as you may find him.

MURDERER 1: He's a traitor.

SON: You lie, you shaggy-haired villain!

MURDERER 1 *(stabbing him)*: What, you egg!
You son of a traitor!

SON: He has killed me, Mother.
Run away, I pray you!

(**Son** dies. **Lady Macduff** exits, crying "Murder!"
Murderers exit, following her.)

Scene ❸ 🎧19

(England. Before the king's palace. **Malcolm** and **Macduff** enter.)

MALCOLM: Let us seek out some lonely shade
And weep there until our tears are gone.

MACDUFF: Let us instead pick up our swords,
And march to our downfallen country.
Each new morning, new widows howl,
New orphans cry, new sorrows hit heaven.
Heaven echoes in sympathy with Scotland,
Yelling out the same cries of sorrow.

MALCOLM: I'll cry for what is happening,
But what I can change, I will.
You may speak the truth.
You once loved this tyrant,
Whose name blisters our tongues.
He has not touched you yet. That makes me
Think that you might still be loyal to him.
Perhaps you plan to win favors from him
By betraying me—a poor, innocent lamb—
To appease an angry god.

MACDUFF: I am not treacherous!

MALCOLM: But Macbeth is.

A good and virtuous nature might act
Dishonorably at a king's command.
But I beg your pardon for these thoughts.
What you are, my thoughts cannot change.

MACDUFF: I have lost my hopes.

MALCOLM:: I have wondered why you left your
Wife and child, those strong knots of love,
Without saying goodbye. Still, I have no
Reason to mistrust you. You may be
Just and true, no matter what I fear.

MACDUFF: Bleed, bleed, poor country!
Great tyranny! Farewell, my lord.
I would not be the villain that you suspect
For all the space in the tyrant's grasp!

MALCOLM: Do not be offended.
I am not in absolute fear of you.
Our country suffers under Macbeth.
Each day a gash is added to her wounds.
I will find support for my cause.
In fact, the King of England has offered
Many thousands to help me. But, for all this,

When I shall tread upon the tyrant's head, or
Wear it on my sword, still my poor country
Will have more troubles than it had before.
It may suffer more, in more ways than ever,
By him who wears the crown after Macbeth.

MACDUFF: Who would he be?

MALCOLM: I mean myself. I know my faults.
When others see them, evil Macbeth
Will look as pure as snow.
The state will regard him as a lamb,
Compared to my endless harms.

MACDUFF: Nobody could top Macbeth in evils!

MALCOLM: I grant that he is brutal, lustful,
Greedy, false, deceitful, and violent.
He smacks of every sin that has a name.
But there's no bottom—none—to my evil.
Your wives, your daughters, your maids, and
Your old women could not satisfy my lust.
Better Macbeth than such a one to reign.

MACDUFF: Such lust is not natural.
It has been the cause of great unhappiness
And the fall of many kings. But fear not

To take what is yours. You could enjoy
The company of many willing women.

MALCOLM: That is not my only failing.
I am also greedy. If I were king,
I would take the nobles' lands,
Demand this one's jewels, that one's house.
The more I got, the more I would want.
Eventually, I'd create unfair quarrels
With the good and loyal,
Destroying them for wealth.

MACDUFF: This greed is worse than young lust.
It has been the sword that killed many kings.
Yet do not fear. Scotland has much wealth
To satisfy you without harming anyone.
All your faults can be tolerated,
Considering your virtues.

MALCOLM: But I have none. The graces that are
Becoming to a king—justice, honesty,
Moderation, stability, generosity, mercy,
Humility, devotion, patience, courage—
I have none of them. Instead, I lean
Toward crime, showing it in many ways.

No, if I had power, I would upset the
Universal peace, confuse all unity on earth.

MACDUFF: Oh, Scotland, Scotland!

MALCOLM: If such a one is fit to rule, speak.
I am as I have spoken.

MACDUFF: Fit to rule? No, not to live!
Oh, miserable nation!
With a bloodthirsty tyrant on the throne,
When shall you see healthy days again,
If the rightful heir is not fit to rule?
Malcolm, your royal father, Duncan,
Was a most sainted king. The queen who
Was your mother lived a life of daily prayer.
Farewell! These evils that you confess
Have banished me from Scotland.
Oh, my country! Your hope ends here!

MALCOLM: Macduff, your noble passion
For Scotland has shown me your honor
And proven to me that you are trustworthy.
The evil Macbeth has often tried to win me
Into his power by offers of women,
Power, and riches—but you did not.
I now assure you that the vices I named

Are strangers to me. I have never even
Been with a woman. I have never lied.
I have hardly even wanted what was mine.
At no time have I broken my faith,
Nor betrayed anyone.
I delight no less in truth than in life.
My first lie was to tell you that I was evil.
What I truly am is this: I am yours,
And my poor country's, to command.
All I want is to serve my country well.
In fact, before you got here, an
English general, with 10,000 warlike men,
Ready for battle, was leaving for Scotland.
We'll go together! But why are you silent?

MACDUFF: Such welcome and unwelcome news
At once! It's hard to take it all in.
See, who comes here?

MALCOLM: I do not recognize him.

(**Ross** enters.)

MACDUFF: Gentle cousin, welcome to England.

MALCOLM: I know him now! I've been away
From Scotland too long. May that soon end!

ROSS: Sir, may it be so.

MACDUFF: Is Scotland still the same?

ROSS: Alas, poor country—
Almost afraid to know itself! It cannot
Now be called our mother, but our grave.
Sighs, groans, and shrieks tear the air.
Violence and sorrow are everywhere.
The bell for the dead rings so often that
No one even asks who has died.
Good men's lives end
Before the flowers in their caps wither.
They die before they have time to get sick.

MALCOLM: What's the newest grief?

ROSS: Hour-long news is already old.
Each minute brings a new one.

MACDUFF: How is my wife?

ROSS: Why, well and at peace.

MACDUFF: And all my children?

ROSS: They were at peace when I left them.

MACDUFF: Don't be so stingy with your words!
What's happening in Scotland?

ACT 4
SCENE 3

ROSS: I've heard that many worthy Scots
Have taken up arms against the tyrant.
I believe this rumor is true, because I saw
The tyrant's soldiers out marching.
We need help now.
(to Malcolm): If only you were in Scotland,
Soldiers would follow you. Even
Women would fight to get rid of Macbeth.

MALCOLM: Tell them that we are coming.
The King of England has lent us
Good Siward and 10,000 men.
An older and better soldier
Cannot be found anywhere.

ROSS: I wish I had good news of my own.
But my words should be howled out
In the desert air, where no one would hear.

MACDUFF: What is your news?
The general cause? Or is it a private grief
For one person alone?

ROSS: Every honest mind shares in the woe,
Though the main part is about you alone.

MACDUFF: If it concerns me, you must tell me.
  Quickly, let me have it!

ROSS: Do not let your ears hate my tongue,
  For I shall fill them with the heaviest sound
  That they have ever heard.

MACDUFF: I can guess at what you will say.

ROSS: Your castle was surprised,
  Your wife and babes savagely slaughtered.
  I cannot tell you anymore details,
  For I fear it would kill you.

MALCOLM: Merciful heaven! Macduff,
  Give words to your sorrow! The grief
  That does not speak whispers to the heart
  And tells it to break.

MACDUFF: My children, too?

ROSS: Wife, children, servants—
  All that could be found.

MACDUFF: And I had to be away!
  My wife was killed, too?

ROSS: I have said so.

MALCOLM: Be comforted.
Let's cure this deadly grief with revenge.

MACDUFF: But Macbeth has no children.
All my pretty ones? Did you say all? All?
My pretty children and their mother
At one fell swoop?

MALCOLM: Take revenge for this like a man.

MACDUFF: I must also feel it as a man.
I cannot stop thinking about those
Who were most precious to me.
Did heaven look on, and not help them?
They were killed because of me—
Not for their faults, but for mine.
May heaven rest them now!

MALCOLM: Let this sharpen your sword.
Turn your grief into anger.
Blunt not your heart—enrage it!

MACDUFF: Gentle heavens, without delay
Bring me face to face
With this fiend of Scotland.
Set him within my sword's length.
If he escapes, may heaven forgive him!

MALCOLM: That's the right idea! Come, let's go
to the king. The army is ready.
All we need is his permission to leave.
Macbeth is like fruit ripe on the tree,
Ready for shaking.
Receive what cheer you may;
The night is long that never finds the day.

(**All** exit.)

ACT 4
SCENE 3

ACT 5

Summary

馬克白夫人發瘋了，她的醫生表示愛莫能助。

在當希南山附近，馬爾康和麥德夫領軍準備進攻。馬爾康要他的軍隊躲在伯南樹林後，以砍下枝葉作為掩護。當馬克白準備回擊時，他接到馬克白夫人去世的消息，並聽說伯南樹林正往當希南山移動，他記起女巫的預言：「馬克白永遠不會被打敗，除非柏南樹林移到當希南」，馬克白感到害怕。

接著，他又想起女巫的另一個預言：「沒有任何女人所生者能傷害得了馬克白」，因而再度感到安心，但他隨後發現麥德夫並非以尋常方式所生。在決戰中，麥德夫殺了馬克白，之後，馬爾康成為蘇格蘭國王。

Scene ❶

(Dunsinane. A room in the castle. A **doctor** and a **gentlewoman** enter.)

GENTLEWOMAN: Since his majesty went into the field with the army, I have seen her do it many times. She rises from bed, takes out a paper, folds it, writes on it, and reads it. Then she seals it and again returns to bed. And she does all this while she is fast asleep.

DOCTOR: Has she said anything?

GENTLEWOMAN: Many things, sir, which I would rather not report.

DOCTOR: You may tell me. In fact, you should.

GENTLEWOMAN: No. I have no witness to back me up. Look—here she comes!

(**Lady Macbeth** enters, carrying a candle.)

That is just how she looks. See, she's fast asleep. Watch her. Stand close.

DOCTOR: How did she get that candle?

GENTLEWOMAN: By her command, she always has light by her bedside.

DOCTOR: Look, her eyes are open!

GENTLEWOMAN: Yes, but she sees nothing.

DOCTOR: Watch how she rubs her hands!

GENTLEWOMAN: Yes, she seems to be washing her hands. I have seen her do this for 15 minutes at a time.

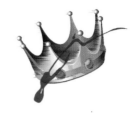

LADY MACBETH: Still, here's a spot.

DOCTOR: Listen, she speaks! I will write down what comes from her, to remember it better.

LADY MACBETH: Out, damned spot! Out, I say! One o'clock, two o'clock. Why, then, it's time to do it. My lord, we need not fear who knows it, for nobody can challenge our power now. Yet who would have thought the old man would have had so much blood in him?

DOCTOR: Do you hear that?

LADY MACBETH: The Thane of Fife had a wife. Where is she now? What, will these hands never be clean? No more of that, my lord, no more of that. You'll ruin everything with your startled movements.

DOCTOR *(to Lady Macbeth)*: You seem to know things you should not know.

LADY MACBETH *(her hand to her nose)*: Here's the smell of the blood still. *(sighing):* All the perfumes of Arabia will not sweeten this little hand.

DOCTOR: What a groan! Her heart is heavy.

GENTLEWOMAN: I would not have such a heart
  in my body for anything!

DOCTOR: This disease is beyond my practice.

LADY MACBETH: Wash your hands. Do not look
  so pale. I tell you—Banquo's buried!
  He cannot return from his grave. To bed!
  Oh! There's knocking at the gate.
  Come, come? Give me your hand.
  What's done cannot be undone.
  To bed, to bed, to bed.

(Lady Macbeth exits.)

DOCTOR: Will she go to bed now?

GENTLEWOMAN: Right away.

DOCTOR: I have heard people whispering
  About evil deeds done here.
  She needs divine help—not mine!
  Look after her. And now, good night.
  What I have seen has amazed my sight.
  I think, but I dare not speak.

(Both exit.)

Scene ❷ 🎧

(The country near Dunsinane. Drums sound. Enter **Menteith**, **Caithness**, **Angus**, **Lennox**, and **soldiers**.)

MENTEITH: The English army is near,
    Led by Malcolm, Siward, and Macduff.
    Desire for revenge burns in them.
    Their dear causes are so just
    That even a dead man would rise to help!

ANGUS: We'll meet them near Birnam Wood.
    That is the way they are coming.

CAITHNESS: Is Donalbain with his brother?

LENNOX: For certain, sir, he is not. I have
    A list of all the men. There is Siward's
    Son, along with many beardless youth
    Who claim they are old enough to fight.

MENTEITH: What is the tyrant Macbeth doing?

CAITHNESS: Protecting his castle, Dunsinane.
    Some say he's mad. Others, who
    Hate him less, call it brave fury.

ANGUS: Now he feels his secret murders
    Sticking on his hands!

ACT 5
SCENE
2

Now small revolts challenge him daily.

Those he commands move only because

He commands it—not because of their

　　love for him.

His title now hangs loose about him,

Like a giant's robe on a dwarfish thief.

CAITHNESS: Well, let's march on

To give obedience where it is truly owed.

We will soon meet Malcolm, the medicine

That will cure Scotland and heal us all.

LENNOX: Yes, let's march on to Birnam Wood.

(**All** exit, marching.)

Scene **3** 🎧22

(Dunsinane. A room in the castle. **Macbeth**, the **doctor**, and **attendants** enter.)

MACBETH: Bring me no more reports.

Until Birnam Wood moves to Dunsinane,

I have nothing to fear. What is Malcolm?

Was he not born of woman? The spirits

That know the future have told me this:

"No man of woman born shall harm

Macbeth."

(A **servant** enters.)

ACT 5
SCENE 3

What do you want, you pale-faced goose?

SERVANT: There are 10,000—

MACBETH: Geese, villain?

SERVANT: Soldiers, sir.

MACBETH: Why does that scare you,

You lily-livered boy? What soldiers, fool?

SERVANT: The English force, your majesty.

MACBETH: Take your face away from here!

(**Servant** exits.)

I am sick at heart. This battle will either

Secure my throne or overthrow me.

I have lived long enough. My youth is over.

That which should accompany old age,

Such as honor, love, obedience, friends,

I must not expect to have. Instead,

I have men who obey me out of fear.

(to the doctor): How is your patient, Doctor?

DOCTOR: Her body is well enough, my lord.

But her mind is troubled with visions

That keep her from her rest.

MACBETH: Cure her of that.

Can you not minister to a sick mind,

Pluck from the memory a deep sorrow, and

Erase the written troubles of the brain?

Clean out the dangerous stuff

That weighs upon her heart

With some sweet medicine of forgetting!

DOCTOR: In cases like this, the patient

Must minister to himself.

MACBETH: Throw medicine to the dogs!

I'll have none of it.

Doctor, the thanes are all leaving me.

If you can find the disease that is troubling
My land, bring her back to a healthy state.

DOCTOR: My good lord, I wish I could.

MACBETH: I will not fear death and pain,
Until Birnam Wood comes to Dunsinane.

(**All** exit except the **doctor**.)

DOCTOR: If I were away from Dunsinane,
Free and clear,
No amount of profit could bring me here.

(**Doctor** exits.)

Scene ❹ 🎧23

(Country near Birnam Wood. Drums sound. **Malcolm**, **old Siward** and **his son**, **Macduff**, **Menteith**, **Angus**, **Caithness**, **Lennox**, **Ross**, and **soldiers** march up.)

SIWARD: What wood is this before us?

MENTEITH: The wood of Birnam.

MALCOLM: Let every soldier cut down a branch
   And carry it before him. That way, we will
   Hide our great numbers, and cause the spies
   To err in reporting back to Macbeth.

SOLDIERS: It shall be done.

SIWARD: We hear that Macbeth is still in
   Dunsinane, waiting there for us.

MALCOLM: It's his main hope, for he knows
   That his men can more easily desert him
   On the battlefield than in the castle.
   None serve him but those who are forced to.
   Their hearts are somewhere else.

MACDUFF: Let us think only of the battle ahead.
Good soldiers are not distracted by rumors.

SIWARD: The time comes that will let us know
What we shall have, and what we shall owe.
Guessing the outcome reveals our hopes,
The issues will be decided by strokes.
So may the battle begin.

(**All** exit, marching.)

ACT 5
SCENE
4

Scene 5 24

(Dunsinane, within the castle. **Macbeth**, **Seyton**, and **soldiers** enter.)

MACBETH: Hang our flags on the outer walls.
Our castle's strength will laugh at them.
Here let them lie until starvation and fever
Eat them up. If they had not been reinforced
With soldiers who deserted us,
We might have been able to meet them
Beard to beard, and beat them back home.

(Wailing cries are heard from within.)

What is that noise?

SEYTON: It is the cry of women, my good lord.

(**Seyton** exits.)

MACBETH: I have almost forgotten
The taste of fears. In the past, my senses
Would have cooled to hear a night shriek,
And my hair would have stood on end.
But I've become so accustomed to horror
That not even such a shriek startles me.

(**Seyton** enters again.)

What was that cry all about?

SEYTON: The queen, my lord, is dead.

MACBETH: She should have died later—when
There would have been time for mourning.
Tomorrow, and tomorrow, and tomorrow,
Creeps on this petty pace from day to day,
To the last syllable of recorded time;
And all our yesterdays have lighted fools
The way to dusty death. Out, out, brief
candle!
Life's but a walking shadow, a poor player
That struts and frets his hour upon the stage
And then is heard no more. It is a tale
Told by an idiot, full of sound and fury,
Signifying nothing.

ACT5
SCENE
5

(A **messenger** enters.)

You came to say something. Say it quickly.

MESSENGER: As I stood my watch upon the hill,
I looked toward Birnam. It seemed
The wood had begun to move!

MACBETH: If you are lying, you shall be hanged
Upon the nearest tree until you starve.

111

If your words are true,
I do not care if you do the same to me.
Now I doubt the words of the Vision
That makes lies sound like truth:
"Macbeth shall never be beaten until
Birnam Wood comes to Dunsinane Hill."
You say a wood moves toward Dunsinane?
Every man take up arms! Prepare to fight!
Ring the alarms! Blow, wind! Come, attack!
At least we'll die with armor on our back.

(**All** exit.)

(A plain before the castle. Drums sound. **Malcolm**, **old Siward**, **Macduff**, and their **army** enter, carrying tree branches.)

MALCOLM: Now we are near enough.

Throw down your leafy screens

And show who you are.

(to old Siward): You, worthy uncle,

shall lead our first battle,

Along with my cousin, your noble son.

Brave Macduff and I shall lead the others.

ACT 5
SCENE 6

SIWARD: Fare you well.

If we find the tyrant's army tonight,

Let us be beaten, if we fail to fight.

MACDUFF: Make all our trumpets speak—

Give them the breath

To loudly sing of blood and death.

(**All** exit.)

Scene 7

(Another part of the plain. **Macbeth** enters.)

MACBETH: I am like a bear tied to a stake.
I cannot run, but, bearlike, I must fight.
Who is he that was not born of woman?
He is the one I must fear—or nobody.

(**Young Siward** enters.)

YOUNG SIWARD: What is your name?

MACBETH: My name's Macbeth.

YOUNG SIWARD: The devil himself could not
Say a name more hateful to my ear.

MACBETH: No, nor more fearful.

YOUNG SIWARD: You lie, hated tyrant!
With my sword, I'll prove it.

(They fight, and **young Siward** is killed.)

MACBETH: You were born of woman!
At swords I smile and all weapons scorn,
When taken up by man of woman born.

(**Macbeth** exits. Young Siward's body is removed from the stage. **Macduff** enters.)

MACDUFF: Tyrant, show your face!

If you are killed by someone other than me,

The ghosts of my wife and children will

Haunt me forever. I will not strike your

Wretched soldiers, who fight for money.

Either it's you, Macbeth,

Or I shall put my sword away unused.

Judging by all the noise, you should be close.

Let me find him, Fortune! I beg for no more.

(**Macduff** exits. **Malcolm** and **old Siward** enter.)

SIWARD: This way, my lord.

The castle has been surrendered.

The noble thanes are winning the war!

Victory soon declares itself yours.

There is little left to do.

MALCOLM: We have met with some foes

Who now fight on our side.

SIWARD: Enter, sir, the castle.

(**All** exit.)

Scene ⑧ 🎧 ⟨27⟩

(Another part of the field. **Macbeth** enters.)

MACBETH: Why should I kill myself with my
Own sword, just because we are losing?
While I see live enemies,
The gashes would be better on them.

(**Macduff** enters.)

MACDUFF: Turn, you villain, turn!

MACBETH: Of all the men here,
I have avoided you. Get back, back!
My soul is too heavy
With your blood already.

MACDUFF: I have no words for you—
My voice is in my sword. You are
A bloodier villain than words can say!

(They fight.)

MACBETH: You are wasting your efforts.
It would be easier for you to cut the air
With your sword than to make me bleed!
Let your blade fall on men you can harm.
I live a charmed life, which will not yield
To a man born of woman.

MACDUFF: Despair of your charm!
Let the devil whom you still serve
Tell you this: Macduff was ripped
From his mother's womb early.
I was not born in the normal way.

MACBETH: Cursed be the tongue that says so,
For it has made my courage fail!
Those deceiving fiends are liars.
They fool us with double meanings.
I won't fight with you.

MACDUFF: Then give up, coward—
And live to be the sideshow of the time!
We'll have your picture painted on a pole,
As we do with our rarer monsters.
Under it we'll write, "Here is the tyrant."

MACBETH: I will not give up,
To kiss the ground at young Malcolm's feet,
And be taunted by the commoners.
So Birnam Wood has come to Dunsinane,
And you were not born of a woman!
Still I will fight to the last. Before my body,
I hold my warlike shield. Fight on, Macduff,
And cursed be he who first cries, "Enough!"

(**They** exit, fighting. Drums sound, and **Malcolm**, **old Siward**, **Ross, Lennox**, **Angus, Caithness, Menteith**, and **soldiers** enter.)

MALCOLM: Oh, that our missing friends
    Had arrived here safely!

SIWARD: Some must die in battle. And yet,
    It looks as if we lost very few soldiers.

MALCOLM: Macduff is missing, and your son.

ROSS: Your son, my lord, was killed in battle.
    He lived only until he was a man,
    Then like a man he died.

SIWARD: You say he is dead?

SERVANT: Yes. Your reason for sorrow
    Must not be measured by his worth,
    For then it would have no end.

SIWARD: Were his wounds on the front?

ROSS: Yes, on the front of his body.

SIWARD: Why, then, he died bravely,
    Facing his enemy.
    If I had as many sons as I have hairs,
    I would not wish them a fairer death.
    And so, God be with him.

(**Macduff** enters, carrying Macbeth's head.)

MACDUFF *(to Malcolm):* Hail, king! See this,
The tyrant's cursed head. We are now free.
Hail, King of Scotland!

ALL: Hail, King of Scotland!

(Trumpets sound.)

MALCOLM: I shall not waste any time before
Rewarding all of you for your efforts today.
My thanes and kinsmen, from this day on,
You are earls, the first named in Scotland.
We shall soon call our exiled friends home,
And bring to trial the cruel ministers
Of this dead butcher and his fiendish queen,
Who, they say, took her own life.
So, thanks to all of you whom
We invite to see us crowned at Scone.

(Trumpets sound. **All** exit.)

中文翻譯

英文內文 P. 004

簡介

在西元一零四零年，馬克白與班珂這兩位大戰告捷的將領，在蘇格蘭一處石南叢生的荒野遇見三名神祕的女巫。

這些女巫預知馬克白終將成為蘇格蘭國王，她們告訴班珂他的兒子們也會坐上王座。

在妻子的慫恿之下，馬克白殺死了鄧肯國王，篡奪大位。惟恐女巫們的後半段預言會成真，馬克白殺死了班珂。

當鄧肯的兒子馬爾康舉兵反抗馬克白時，馬克白夫人不堪良心的譴責而自戕。隨後，馬克白被麥德夫殺死，馬爾康繼位為國王。

出場人物

鄧肯：蘇格蘭國王

馬爾康與道南班：國王的兒子

馬克白：國王軍隊的將領

班珂：國王軍隊的將領

雷諾克斯、羅斯、麥德夫、安格斯、凱瑟尼斯、曼泰斯：
　　蘇格蘭貴族

佛良斯：班珂的兒子

西華德：諾森伯蘭伯爵，英格蘭軍隊的將領

西華德之子：西華德的兒子

西登：馬克白的隨從

男孩：麥德夫的兒子

英格蘭醫生、蘇格蘭醫生、士兵、腳夫、老人

馬克白夫人

麥德夫夫人：馬克白夫人的侍女

三名女巫

領主們、紳士們、軍官們、士兵們、殺手們、侍從們與信差們

班珂的鬼魂與其他幾位鬼魂

第一幕

● 第一場 ——————————————————— P. 007

（荒郊野外，雷電交加；三名女巫上。）

女巫一：你我三人何時能再相見？在雷電交加時或是在雨天？

女巫二：待這混亂結束，等戰爭分出勝負。

女巫三：在日落前的下午。

女巫一：我們要在何處見面？

女巫二：在石南叢生的荒野。

女巫三：我們會在那兒見到馬克白。

女巫一：現在先回家吧。

一起：美麗即是醜陋，醜陋即是美麗——飛越迷霧和混濁的空氣。

（女巫們消失。）

● 第二場 ——————————————————— P. 008

（在福雷斯附近的一處軍營，舞台後方傳來警報聲；鄧肯國王、馬爾康、道南班與雷諾克斯上，隨從們陪侍在側；他們遇見一名流血的士兵。）

鄧肯：那位流血的人是誰？從他的外表看來，他能告訴我們目前的戰況。

馬爾康：此人是幫我殺出重圍免受俘虜的士兵。（對士兵：）你好，英勇的弟兄！目前的戰況如何？

士兵：馬克白的劍被染紅了，他在戰場上殺出重圍！最後和惡徒麥克唐納正面交鋒，他並未握手言和或道別；反之，從腹部至下顎割得他肚破腸流，將他的首級高掛在城牆上。

鄧肯：喔，英勇又高尚的表親！

士兵：隨後從東方傳來了麻煩。請聽我道來，蘇格蘭國王，聽好了！當叛軍開始逃跑時，挪威領主逮到可乘之機，在得到新送達的軍械和增援的人馬之後，發動了新一波的攻擊行動。

鄧肯：我軍將領馬克白與班珂豈不聞之驚慌？

士兵：是的——但如同麻雀欲嚇跑老鷹，或野兔使獅子驚慌失措！陛下，他們宛如裝填雙倍火藥的大砲一般！因為敵軍每發動一次進攻，他們就還之以兩回合反擊。但我已然暈眩，我的傷勢嚴重！

鄧肯：你的話語和傷口都訴說著你的榮譽。（對隨從們：）去吧，帶他去就醫。（**士兵們下，隨從們尾隨而出。**）（對馬爾康：）來者何人？

馬爾康：羅斯領主閣下。

（**羅斯上。**）

羅斯：國王陛下萬福！

鄧肯：你從何處而來，領主閣下？

羅斯：來自伐夫，偉大的國王陛下，那裡滿天飛揚著挪威軍旗，我國人民無不驚惶。挪威國王親自帶領千軍萬馬，向我軍宣戰。對本國不忠的考德領主臨陣倒戈，轉而援助挪威國王。最後，馬克白全副武裝，以更驚人的氣勢向他挑戰。劍鋒相對，短兵相接，馬克白打得他潰不成軍，終於我軍大獲全勝。

鄧肯：可喜可賀！

羅斯：如今，挪威國王史威諾意欲投降。我們不准他讓陣亡將士下葬，除非他先支付我們一萬元的降金。

鄧肯：今後考德領主再也不得背叛我國！快去，即刻處死他，將他原有的封號賜給馬克白。

羅斯：陛下之命我必從之。

鄧肯：他輸掉的，即是馬克白閣下所贏得的。

（全體下。）

●第三場 ————————————— P. 011

（在福雷斯的一處荒野，閃電大作；三名女巫上；舞台後方傳來鼓聲。）

女巫一：鼓聲隆隆！馬克白已現行蹤。

一起：攜手同行的女巫們，在海陸航行跋涉的旅人們，在各處奔波往返。到你那兒三趟、到我這兒三趟，再跑個三趟總共是九趟。好了！咒語已然施下。

（馬克白與班珂上。）

馬克白：如此慘烈又美好的一天，是我前所未見。

班珂：到福雷斯還要多遠？（他看到女巫們。）這幾個人究竟是誰？如此面容憔悴、衣著怪誕，看上去不似凡人，卻又存在於這世間。

馬克白：有什麼話就說吧。來者何人？

女巫一：馬克白，葛萊密斯領主萬福！

女巫二：馬克白，考德領主萬福！

女巫三：馬克白萬福！你今後將登基為王！

班珂：馬克白，你何以退縮？你為何恐懼聽上去如此美好之事？（對女巫們：）以真相之名，你們是幻想？抑或是外表顯現的那樣？你們見著我這位貴族友人，對他的未來給了美好的預測，細述他將擁有高尚的頭銜和王室的位階，為何對我卻無隻字片言？倘若你們能窺探時間的種籽，告訴我哪些能生、哪些不能，請告訴我吧，我不求你們幫忙，也不害怕你們偏袒或憎恨。

女巫一：萬福！

女巫二：萬福！

女巫三：萬福！

女巫一：不及馬克白，卻又更偉大。

女巫二：不甚快樂，卻又更快樂。

女巫三：你的眾兒孫們終將成為國王，然而你卻不會是。所以，馬克白與班珂萬福！

女巫一：馬克白與班珂萬福！

馬克白：請繼續把話說完。自從家父過世之後，我的確成為葛萊密斯領主，但我何以又是考德領主？考德領主此刻正活得好好的，他是富可敵國的紳士。我既不可能是考德領主，更不可能成為國王。說吧，你們是從何得知如此怪異的消息？又為何在這石南叢生的荒野之中攔下我們，說了這些問候和預言之語？我命令你們據實以告！

（**女巫們消失。**）

班珂：大地沸騰冒泡，一如沸水；此番謬言想必也會如氣泡般破滅。瞧！她們消失不見了！

馬克白：憑空消失，看似真實卻如氣息般消融在風中。但願她們能留下！

班珂：她們是真的來過嗎？還是我們吃了某些食物禁錮了我們的理智？

馬克白：你的兒孫們將成為國王。

班珂：你將成為國王！

馬克白：而且也是考德領主。她們不是這麼說的嗎？

班珂：是的，她們所言正是如此。（聽見聲音。）來者何人？

（羅斯與安格斯上。）

羅斯：馬克白，國王已然聞悉你凱旋的喜訊！聽聞你在戰場上對抗叛軍的英勇事蹟，陛下又驚又喜。你捍衛國土居功甚偉，眾人皆大力讚賞，陛下喜聞你在前線作戰無所畏懼。

安格斯：國王陛下要給你更大的獎勵，即刻賜封你為考德領主。容我先行道賀，領主萬福！這個頭銜是閣下的了。

班珂：難道那些女巫之言屬實？

馬克白：但是考德領主依然健在！何以用他人的頭銜賜封於我？

安格斯：原本的考德領主確實還活著，但是他活該要丟了性命。他被指控倒戈投向挪威陣營，或是可能祕密援助挪威國王，也許他做這兩件事是為了毀滅自己的國家；他是如何辦到的我不得而知，然而這些指控已是罪證確鑿，他也招認犯下叛國罪，如今死刑已然宣判。

馬克白（竊語）：葛萊密斯領主，如今又是考德領主！最偉大的頭銜亦將加諸於我！（對班珂：）難道你不希望兒孫能成為國王？畢竟告知我將成為考德領主之人，亦做出如是的應許之言。

班珂：倘若我們全盤相信這些預言，那麼你可能也會成為國王。但是說來奇怪，邪巫經常為了陷我們於罪，告知我們難

126

毛蒜皮的小實話，由小處搏取我們的信任，只等著來日在大事上陷我們於萬劫不復。（對羅斯與安格斯：）表親們，請借一步說話。

馬克白（竊語）：她們的預言已有兩則成真！更偉大的預言告知我將成為國王，似乎是個喜訊。（對羅斯與安格斯：）多謝二位。（竊語：）這神祕的預言不知道是好或壞。若是惡兆，為何先據實以告、讓我功成名就？因我確實成了考德領主。若是好兆頭，為何有可怕的念頭讓我胸口心跳加快？想像出來的駭人情景，比真正的恐懼更令人害怕。殺害國王的念頭掠過我的腦海，令我惶恐不安到快要窒息，然而除此之外的一切對我而言似乎都不真實。

班珂（對羅斯與安格斯）：瞧瞧馬克白，他似乎恍惚出神了。

馬克白（竊語）：倘若我命中注定要成為國王，那麼命運終將為我加冕——即使我什麼也不做。

班珂（對羅斯與安格斯）：馬克白受封了新頭銜，如同新衣裳一般，要等穿了一陣子才會合身。

馬克白（竊語）：無論未來將會如何，再忙亂的時日也總會過去。

班珂：馬克白閣下，就等你啟程了。

馬克白：請原諒我，我方才想得出神了。我們這就去面見國王。（對班珂：）想想之前發生的事，稍後等我們都思考周全了，再來好好聊聊這件事吧。

班珂：樂意之至。

馬克白：在此之前，罷了！走吧，朋友們。

（全體下。）

（福雷斯，皇宮；鄧肯國王、馬爾康、道南班、雷諾克斯與隨從們上。）

鄧肯：考德領主是否已遭處決？官員們都回來了嗎？

馬爾康：還沒有，陛下，但是我問過其中一人，他親眼看著考德領主死去。他對自己的叛逆罪坦承不諱，然後哀求陛下的寬恕。他一生行事未曾如臨終前那般得體；他死時彷彿早已演練好，將他在世間最珍愛的一切皆視如草芥一般拋棄了。

鄧肯：哎呀！知人知面不知心！他生前是朕非常信任的紳士。
（馬克白、班珂、羅斯與安格斯上。）（對馬克白：）喔，最高尚的表親！朕欠你的恩情此生無以回報。

馬克白：為陛下效忠即是我最大的報酬，陛下只需領受我們的效忠即可，保護陛下的安全是我們的職責所在。

鄧肯：朕給你的獎賞才只是開始而已，現在朕要繼續賜封使你飛黃騰達。至於你，班珂閣下，你也理應接受封賞，就讓朕擁抱你，讓你貼近朕的胸膛。

班珂：為陛下效勞是我的榮幸。

鄧肯：朕的兒子們，諸位親戚和領主，以及朕身邊所有的親信，請仔細聽好：朕要將王位傳給長子馬爾康；從今爾後，他的封號就是坎伯蘭王子。不僅他要接受賜封，貴族封銜有如繁星一般，凡是值得之人皆應如沐星光。現在，就讓我們一同前往因佛尼斯參觀馬克白的城堡吧。

馬克白：我將先行前去，告知內人陛下將親臨探訪的喜訊。（鞠躬。）請容我先行告退。

鄧肯：考德領主閣下！

馬克白（竊語）：坎伯蘭王子！此乃一大阻礙，我若非被它絆倒，就是要從其上一躍而過──因他阻撓了我眼前的路。繁星啊，藏起你們的光芒！切莫讓人窺見我內心深處的暗黑欲望。

（馬克白下。）

鄧肯：是啊，班珂閣下！馬克白的讚美使朕心滿意足，對朕如同一場盛宴，且讓我們跟隨平步青雲的他，並接受他的盛情款待。他是無與比擬的皇室親信！

（全體下。）

●第五場

（因佛尼斯，馬克白的城堡；馬克白夫人上，手裡拿著一封信。）

馬克白夫人（讀信）：「三名女巫證實了她們有預知未來的能力。在她們憑空消失之後，國王派來了幾名信差，他們稱我為『考德領主』——那些女巫亦是如此稱呼我！女巫們還說：『馬克白萬福！他假以時日必將登基為王。』我想與你分享此一喜訊，我最親愛偉大的夫人，讓你也能即刻得知這被應許的大好消息！此事務必保密，後會有期。」（評論信件內容：）你已是葛萊密斯領主，如今又成為考德領主。對你的預言將會悉數成真，然而你天生的性格令我憂懼。邁向成功最快的捷徑，將被你充滿良善的人性阻撓。你渴望成就大業，你野心勃勃，但是你在性格上卻欠缺必要的冷酷無情。你內心深刻渴望得到的，你會用誠實的方法達到目的，不會不擇手段行不誠實之事。你需要有人對你說：「倘若你想要這樣，你就必須那麼做。」快快返家，好讓我將我的氣魄灌入你耳中！讓我推你一把，用我強而有力的言語克服眼前重重阻礙，送你直上國王的寶座。命運和邪巫預言皆已注定你將繼承大統。

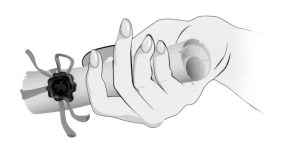

（一名僕人上。）

馬克白夫人：你帶來什麼信息？

僕人：國王今晚將大駕親臨。

馬克白夫人：你少在這兒胡說八道！我夫君不是正和陛下在一起嗎？若真如此，他早該告知我事先做好準備。

僕人：請夫人相信我所言句句屬實，領主閣下即將歸來，捎來信息的差使已經奔波疲累，剩下的力氣只夠他傳遞此一口信。

馬克白夫人：好好照顧他，他帶來的可是天大的好消息。（僕人下。）渡烏通報著鄧肯來日無多的噩耗，反覆嘶叫到已經沙啞。來啊，邪靈們，讓我從頭到腳充滿最致命的殘酷！讓我的血變得濃稠，除去我所有惻隱和感傷的情緒，不讓任何的婦人之仁動搖我邪惡的預謀。來啊，陰暗的夜晚！藏身於地獄最黑暗的濃霧籠罩中，不讓我的利刃看到它刺出的傷口，也不讓老天從黑夜屏幕中探頭高喊：「且慢！且慢！」（馬克白上。）偉大的葛萊密斯領主！高尚的考德領主！更甚者，備受萬民擁戴亦指日可待！你的來信讓我知悉所有的消息！我此刻即可感受到未來的榮華！

馬克白：我最親愛的夫人，鄧肯今晚會大駕親臨。

馬克白夫人：他預備何時離開？

馬克白：明天，他是這麼打算的。

馬克白夫人：喔，他再也見不到明天的太陽！我的領主，你的面容好似一本書，能讓旁人有奇怪的解讀，欺瞞時間、模擬時間；你要用眼神、手勢和言語來歡迎他。看似無辜純潔的花朵，實際上是潛伏於其下的毒蛇。我們要盛情歡迎他的到來，今晚這樁大事就交給我來張羅吧，我會處理好一切！讓我們未來的日日夜夜皆以國王與王后的身分度過。

馬克白：此事稍後再談。

馬克白夫人：你且保持冷靜，切莫做出招人疑心之舉，其他的事就交給我吧。

（兩人下。）

●第六場 P. 027

（在馬克白的城堡門口；鄧肯國王、馬爾康、道南班、班珂、雷諾克斯、麥德夫、羅斯、安格斯與眾僕人上。）

鄧肯：此座城堡的環境頗為怡人，溫和甜美的空氣令人神清氣爽。

班珂（指向一隻鳥）：這種鳥經常在空氣清新之處築巢。

（馬克白夫人上。）

鄧肯：看啊，看啊，是我們尊榮的女主人！感謝你為我們今日的來訪，煩費周章地進行準備。

馬克白夫人：即使我們做足雙倍的準備，甚至再付出雙倍的努力，也比不上陛下大駕光臨寒舍讓我們蓬蓽生輝啊。

鄧肯：把你的手給朕，帶朕去見見我最親信的男主人。

（全體下。）

● 第七場 ——————————————— P. 028

（在馬克白的城堡內；馬克白上。）

馬克白： 倘若真要下手，最好速戰速決，真希望刺殺行動就能
終結一切！倘若真能刺殺成功，那就更好了，但是我們仍然
要面對天譴，報應使我們在謀害人命之前裹足。鄧肯來此
乃是對我的雙重信任——首先，我是他的親戚和寵臣，因
此更不應該如是待他；其次，我是他的東道主，應該防堵外
人進來刺殺他，而非將利刃握於我自己手中！況且，鄧肯的
天性良善，他勤政愛民的作為宛如天使一般懇求我饒他性
命。我沒有殺害他的好理由，純粹是為了我個人的野心，彷
彿過於急切的騎士似地在跳上馬背時，很可能用力過猛而
從彼側摔落。（馬克白夫人上。）情況如何？

馬克白夫人： 他即將用完晚餐。你何以走出房門外？

馬克白： 他是否要求召見我？

馬克白夫人： 難道你不知他早已提及？

馬克白： 我們的計畫不如就此打住吧。他已賜封予我，亦有形
形色色的人提供我寶貴的建言。我理應接受這些新忠告，
而非急欲棄之如敝屣。

馬克白夫人： 那你對未來的期望又如何？難道野心已然沉睡？
你害怕將心之所欲化為行動嗎？你要畢生當個懦夫讓自己
也瞧不起，只能說「我不敢」而不說「我願意」嗎？你此刻可
比想吃魚、卻又不敢弄濕腳掌的貓。

馬克白： 我懇求你，莫再多言！但凡男人能做的事我都敢做，
然而行為更甚者就稱不上是條漢子了。

馬克白夫人（語氣憤怒）：那你又何必將此狼子野心告知於我？你現在敢做才算是個男人；比你原本做的更多，你就是男人中的男人。來吧——你早已發誓要下手！

馬克白：萬一我們失敗了怎麼辦？

馬克白夫人：只要鼓起足夠的勇氣，我們就不會失敗。等到鄧肯熟睡了，我會給他的兩名守衛飲下烈酒，他們不久便也會睡著，我們再殺死毫無防備的鄧肯，此事輕而易舉。事後嫁禍給兩名酒醉的守衛，將我們的殺人罪行栽贓給他們。

馬克白：好！待我們用鄧肯的血沾染在兩名熟睡的守衛身上，並且用他們隨身的匕首取他性命之後，所有的人都會認定他們就是兇手。

馬克白夫人：有誰會另作他想——尤其我們會在他死時嚎啕哭號？

馬克白：那就這麼決定了。去吧，用最美麗的外表去欺瞞時間，唯有虛偽的面貌才能藏住奸詐的內心。

（他們下。）

第二幕

● 第一場 ——————————————————— P. 033

（馬克白城堡的庭院；班珂、佛良斯與一名僕人帶著火炬上。）

班珂：是何時辰了，孩子？

僕人：已過午夜，閣下。

班珂：天堂也講究節約，因為繁星如同燭光一般全都熄滅。我心頭有種沉重如鉛塊的感覺，然而我難以成眠。慈悲的力量，阻止那令我輾轉反覆的邪惡念頭吧！（聽見有聲音：）來者何人？

（馬克白與一名僕人帶著火炬上。）

馬克白：是朋友。

班珂：閣下，何以尚未歇息？國王陛下已經睡下，他心情愉悅，還差人饋贈厚禮予你的部屬們，他稱尊夫人是周到的女主人，語罷便心滿意足地就寢了。

馬克白：未能事先得知陛下將大駕光臨，我惟恐我們招待得不夠周全。

班珂：一切都好。我昨夜夢見那三個怪異的女人，她們給你的第一個預言已然成真！

馬克白：倘若你對我忠心耿耿，待時機成熟時你必能得到榮耀。

班珂：我追求更多榮耀時，不會使之蒙羞。倘若我對你盡忠時也能無愧於心，那我必定會接受你的忠告。

馬克白：那就祝你好夢吧！

班珂：多謝閣下，也祝你好夢！

（班珂、佛良斯與他們的僕人下。）

馬克白（對他的僕人）：轉告我的夫人，準備好我的酒水就鳴鐘示意。（僕人下。）在我面前似乎觸手可及的是一把匕首嗎？刀柄向著我的手？致命的景象，我看得見你，是否也摸得著你？或者你只是一把想像的匕首，我因腦門發熱而產生的假象？我仍然看得見你，如同這把匕首一般真實；現在，我要拔刀出鞘了。（他拔出自己真正的匕首。）你指引我實際應走的道路，我的雙眼是被其他感官所蒙騙，抑或是比其他感官更敏銳？我仍然看得見你，你的刀刃上沾染了原本未有的鮮血。你並非真實存在，這血腥的陰謀令我產生幻覺！此刻，半個世界皆已沉睡死寂，噩夢驚擾了酣睡中的人們。堅實的大地，莫聽我的腳步聲，切莫留意它們往哪兒去，我深恐路面上的石頭會洩露我的行蹤。在我說話的此時，鄧肯仍有氣息；言語吹出冰冷的空氣，冷卻衝動的行徑。（鐘聲響起。）我這就要下手了，鐘聲在召喚我。你別聽了，鄧肯，因為那是召喚你踏進冰冷墳墓的喪鐘。

（馬克白下。馬克白夫人上。）

馬克白夫人：讓他們喝醉的也使我大膽，解他們渴的亦使我著火。聽啊！貓頭鷹的驚聲尖叫，致命的鳴鐘之人道了最後一聲晚安。啊！我看到醉酒的守衛們用鼾聲在嘲弄他們的國王。我在他們的酒裡下了藥，好讓他們無論是生或死，都能酣睡如同死去一般。

馬克白（在舞台後方）：出了什麼事？

馬克白夫人（自言自語）：哎呀！他們已經醒來，而計謀尚未完成。令我們驚慌的是意圖，而非實際行動！我將他們的匕首放在顯眼之處，他不可能沒看見。若非睡夢中的鄧肯看似我的親生父親，我早已親自下手。

（馬克白再上，滿身是血。）

馬克白夫人：我的夫君！

馬克白：我已經下手，難道你沒聽見聲音嗎？

馬克白夫人：我聽見貓頭鷹的尖叫聲和蟋蟀的鳴聲。

馬克白：有一個人在睡夢中大笑，另一個人大喊「殺人！」；他們似乎驚醒了彼此，但是很快就又再睡去。

馬克白夫人：在鄧肯的隔牆房間，睡著另外兩位賓客。

馬克白：一個驚呼「上帝保佑我們！」，另一個説「阿們」。深恐他們看見我這染血的雙手，聽到他們驚恐地喊出「上帝保佑我們！」之時，我卻説不出「阿們」。

馬克白夫人：你就別放在心上了。

馬克白：但是我何以説不出「阿們」？我最迫切需要上帝的保佑，「阿們」二字卻哽在喉頭。

馬克白夫人：這種事做完了就別再多想，否則只會逼瘋自己。

馬克白：我聽見有個聲音大喊：「別再睡了！馬克白已謀殺了睡眠！」唯有清白者才能入睡──睡眠織平憂慮的亂絲，消弭日常煩惱，是受傷心靈的良藥，也是生命筵席上的主餐。

馬克白夫人：你此言是何意？

馬克白：它還在大喊：「不要睡了！」對著全屋子的人大喊。「葛萊密斯謀殺了睡眠，因此考德將不得安眠，馬克白也再也無法入睡！」

馬克白夫人：此話是何人所喊出，我的夫君？你將自己高尚的氣力浪費在如此荒誕的念頭上。快去洗淨你手上的染血證據吧，你為何將這匕首帶在身上？匕首必須留在現場才是。快，放回去！在沉睡的守衛身上沾抹鮮血！

馬克白：我無法回去了，我不願再目睹我的所作所為，那令我感到害怕！

馬克白夫人：懦夫！將匕首交給我吧。沉睡和死亡只是彼此的倒影，唯有孩童才會為之恐懼！我來用他的鮮血塗抹在守衛們的臉上，將此罪栽贓給他們。

（她下，傳來敲門聲。）

馬克白： 那是什麼敲門聲？何以我如此草木皆兵？這雙手是什麼？用盡所有的海水能否洗淨我雙手沾染的鮮血？我手上的血跡足以將碧綠的海水染紅！

（馬克白夫人再上。）

馬克白夫人： 我的雙手和你一樣染了血，然而我以懷著純潔的心為羞恥。

（再傳來敲門聲。）

馬克白夫人： 我在南側入口處聽見敲門聲。我們回房去洗淨雙手吧，此事就這麼簡單！（又傳來敲門聲。）你聽！又傳來敲門聲，快換上你的睡袍，我們要假裝早已睡了，切莫迷失在你的思緒中無法自拔。

馬克白： 我寧可迷失在思緒中，也不想再回頭看自己的犯行。（又傳來敲門聲。）用你的敲門聲吵醒鄧肯吧！但願你能吵醒他！

（兩人下，一名腳夫上；繼續傳來敲門聲。）

腳夫： 是誰在敲門？我這就來了！

（他打開大門，麥德夫與雷諾克斯上。）

麥德夫： 你的主人是否還醒著？喔，是我們的敲門聲吵醒了他。他來了。

（馬克白上，穿著睡袍。）

雷諾克斯： 早安，尊貴的閣下！

馬克白： 早安，兩位！

麥德夫： 領主閣下，國王是否已醒來？

馬克白： 應該還沒有吧。

麥德夫：陛下要我一早來見他，我差點就錯過了他指定的時間。

馬克白：那就是通往他寢室的門。

（麥德夫下。）

雷諾克斯：國王是今天離開嗎？

馬克白：是的，至少他是這麼說的。

雷諾克斯：這一夜很不平靜，我們在睡夢中聽見煙囪傳來風聲，有人說聽見慟哭聲、死亡的怪異尖叫聲，還有興奮與困惑的可怕預示。貓頭鷹徹夜尖聲鳴叫不休，有人說發熱的大地還震動了！

馬克白：這一夜確實不好過。

雷諾克斯：我印象中不曾遇過此般的夜晚。

（麥德夫再上。）

麥德夫（驚惶失措）：喔，可怕、可怕、太可怕了！超乎想像，亦非言語所能形容！

馬克白與雷諾克斯：怎麼回事？

麥德夫：此乃混亂騷動之極致！最可怕的凶案發生在閣下的聖殿中，奪去了陛下的性命。

馬克白：你說什麼——奪去性命？

雷諾克斯：你指的是國王陛下？

麥德夫：去他的寢室親眼一見便知，切莫再要我說下去了！看啊，你們眼見為憑。（麥德夫與雷諾克斯下。）醒來、醒來！鳴響警報的鐘聲！叛逆和謀殺！班珂與道南班！馬爾康！快醒來！從溫柔的睡夢之中醒來吧，那只是死亡的模擬，親眼看看死亡為何物吧！起來、起來，看看這生命毀滅的景象！馬爾康！班珂！快起來看看這駭人的一幕！

（警報鐘聲響起；馬克白夫人再上。）

馬克白夫人：這是怎麼回事？何以發出如此可怕的聲音，吵醒這屋內熟睡的人們？說啊！

麥德夫：喔，高貴的夫人，我所言你不宜聽之。倘若此事對婦人訴說，她聽聞之後會嚇得花容失色。（班珂再上。）喔，班珂、班珂！我們的國王陛下遭人謀害了！

馬克白夫人：哎呀，太慘了！竟在我們屋內？

班珂：無論發生在哪兒都太殘酷了。親愛的麥德夫，我懇求你告訴我這不是真的。

（馬克白、雷諾克斯與羅斯上。）

馬克白：倘若我在事發一小時前死去，我此生就算有福氣。從今爾後人生已無意義，一切皆無異於兒戲，名聲與榮光已死，生命的酒已被斟盡，只剩下渣滓而已。

（馬爾康與道南班上。）

道南班：什麼出了錯？

馬克白：你出了錯──而你卻渾然不知。你血脈的源頭已然停止流動；它的根本起源停止了。

麥德夫：你的父王遭人殺害了。

馬爾康：喔，不！兇手是何人？

雷諾克斯：似乎是他的守衛們下了毒手，他們的雙手和臉上都沾染血跡。我們發現他們置於枕頭上的匕首，上頭的鮮血亦未抹去；切莫再將任何人交給他們看顧。

馬克白：即便如此，我仍然壓抑不住盛怒而殺死他們。

麥德夫：那你為何痛下殺手？

馬克白：何人能在驚愕之餘保有智慧，在盛怒之下保持冷靜，在處於忠憤之際仍保持不偏不倚的態度？無人能做到。我對鄧肯的敬愛凌駕於我的理智之上，我們的國王躺在這兒，他神聖的皮膚上沾滿他尊貴的鮮血。殺人兇手渾身是血地在那兒，他們的匕首上亦是血跡斑斑！但凡敬愛陛下、又有勇氣昭告天下者，都會有如是的反應。

馬克白夫人（昏厥）：救救我！

麥德夫：照看好這位夫人。

馬爾康（向道南班竊語）：何以眾人皆在議論於我們如此重要之事，而我們卻緘口不言？

道南班（向馬爾康竊語）：我們並不安全，你我的命運可能藏在某個隱密之處，隨時會伺機而動衝出來一把抓住我們。我們快逃走吧，擇日再為父王之死而哭泣。

班珂：照看好這位夫人。（*馬克白夫人被人抬出去。*）讓我們都去
更衣著裝吧，然後再回來此地談論這場無比血腥的凶案，
試圖抽絲剝繭以理出頭緒。恐懼與疑慮令我們驚惶，我站
在上帝的偉大引導之下，必將對抗叛逆與邪惡的未知力量。

麥德夫：我亦如是。

全體：我們亦如是。

馬克白：讓我們披上戰甲，在大廳會合吧。

（*除馬爾康與道南班之外，全體下。*）

馬爾康：此刻你我應該如何？我們莫與眾人會合，強作悲傷神
情乃虛偽之人的拿手好戲。我將逃往英格蘭。

道南班：而我將逃往愛爾蘭，你我分頭逃跑才會比較安全。此
時你我所在之處，必定有人是笑裡藏刀；我們的血脈至親
才是最有可能殺害我們之人。

馬爾康：殺人的箭在被射出之後尚未落地，我們最安全的出路
即是避開箭矢之的。你我皆莫與任何人道別，只消偷偷地
離開此地；在慈悲蕩然無存之處，亦無榮耀可言。

（*馬爾康與道南班下。*）

（在馬克白的城堡外面；羅斯與麥德夫上。）

羅斯：可知是何人犯下此殺人罪行？

麥德夫：馬克白方才手刃的兩名守衛。

羅斯：但是他們的動機何在？

麥德夫：他們是受雇於人。國王之子馬爾康與道南班已然
　　　　逃走，眾貴族們皆疑心是他倆所為。

羅斯：此乃違逆天道之舉！他們何以殺死自己的父親？如今看
　　　來，最有可能繼承王位者實屬馬克白。

麥德夫：他已被指名繼任國王，趕赴斯康接受加冕大典。

羅斯：鄧肯的遺體何在？

麥德夫：他的遺體將被抬往斯康，下葬在歷代蘇格蘭國王的
　　　　陵墓中。

羅斯：你也要前往斯康嗎？

麥德夫：不，表親，我將返回伐夫家中。

羅斯：那我將前往斯康。

麥德夫：但願在那兒能一切順利。再會！

羅斯：你也再會。

（羅斯與麥德夫下。）

第三幕

● 第一場 ───────────────── P. 051

（福雷斯，皇宮內的一個房間；班珂上。）

班珂（自言自語）：如今你擁有了一切——國王、考德領主、葛萊密斯領主——那三個怪異女人的預言成真了。倘若她們對你的預言成真，或許她們對我的承諾也將兌現。若真如此，我可以引頸期盼了。好了，莫再多言。

（號角聲響起；馬克白以國王的身分上，馬克白夫人以王后的身分跟隨在後，雷諾克斯、羅斯、眾領主、眾夫人與侍從們亦隨之而上。）

馬克白：今晚將舉辦盛宴，希望閣下務必要來賞光。

班珂：陛下之願我必從之。

馬克白：你今日午後要去騎馬嗎？

班珂：是的，國王陛下。

馬克白：你會騎很遠嗎？

班珂：足以填補此刻到晚餐時間的空檔，陛下。

馬克白：切莫耽擱了赴宴的時辰。

班珂：不會的，陛下。

馬克白：聽說我們那冷血弒父的表親馬爾康和道南班，已分別逃往了英格蘭和愛爾蘭，他們並未自承手刃親父，反而捏造了關於先王之死的荒謬說法以混淆視聽。然而此事我們明日再議。先此道別，等你今夜返回赴宴。佛良斯是否將與你同行？

班珂：是的，國王陛下。

（班珂下；馬克白對其他人說話。）

馬克白：你們可自由活動到今晚七點。為了更周全地招待各位佳賓，下午就讓朕獨處吧。願上帝與你們同在。

（全體下，獨留馬克白與一名僕人。）

馬克白（對僕人）：朕請來的幾個人，他們是否已到？

僕人：是的，陛下，他們已在門外候著。

馬克白：帶他們來見朕。

（僕人下。）

馬克白：繼位為國王不代表什麼，除非地位鞏固了。朕對班珂的恐懼日益加深，他對這王位是一威脅。當女巫們預言我將繼任為王之時，她們稱他的子孫將世代為王。加冕於我頭頂的是毫無意義的王冠，因為假以時日卻不是由朕的兒子來繼位。倘若預言為真，朕謀殺了先王鄧肯，終究只是讓班珂的兒子們繼任為王！此非朕之所願，就讓命運來與我決戰吧。（他聽見聲音。）來者何人？（僕人再上，帶著兩名殺手。）去門外守著等朕的傳喚。（僕人下。）我們不是昨天才談過嗎？

殺手一：是的，陛下。

馬克白：好吧，朕的話你們是否已深思熟慮？你們知道過去為你們帶來不幸的是班珂，而非你們原先懷疑的無辜的朕？

殺手一：陛下已經告知我們。

馬克白：你們能否寬恕？你們是否善良到在他的無情之手毀了你們、讓你們的子女淪為乞丐之後，仍能為他禱告？

殺手一：我們是人啊，陛下。

馬克白：是的，在物種的分類上你們是人，一如獵犬、格力犬、雜種狗、西班牙獵狗、捲毛狗、落水狗和狼犬皆被歸類為「犬」。最好的分類名單說明了速度快慢，野狗、家犬、獵犬之差異，每一種皆有天生具備的特殊才能；而人類亦如是。你們自認高於人類的最低階層嗎？若真如此，我將派給你們一項特別的任務，能從名單上除去你們的敵人，讓你們更得朕之歡心。因為有他的存在，朕就分秒難安；然而在他死後，朕的人生將臻至完美。

殺手二： 陛下，我飽受到世人的打擊，已氣憤到足以不擇手段報復全世界。

殺手一： 我亦如是——早已厭倦了不幸，不想再厄運纏身，拼死也要逮住任何翻身或擺脫困厄的機會。

馬克白： 你們都視班珂為敵人。

兩名殺手： 是的，陛下

馬克白： 他也是朕的敵人。有他存在就無時無刻如同利刃抵住朕的心臟一般，雖然朕只消一聲令下即可除掉他，但是朕不願這麼做。朕與他有些共同的朋友會因他之死而哀悼，而朕需要他們的效忠，因此朕要請求你們的相助。殺了他——但是切莫讓任何人對朕有所疑心！

殺手二： 我們將聽從陛下的吩咐。

馬克白： 今晚必須行動，而且要在城堡之外下手。記住，不得讓人對朕起疑心。只准成功，不許失敗！班珂之子佛良斯將伴隨在側，他的死和他父親的死對朕而言同等重要，他必須在這黑暗的時辰面對命運的操弄。在大門外等候，朕即刻告知進一步的指示。（*殺手們下。*）已經安排好了。班珂，你的靈魂即將飛走；是否將飛上天堂，今晚便可分曉。

（*馬克白下。*）

（馬克白夫人與一名僕人上，走進皇宮的一個房間。）

馬克白夫人：請國王來此見我。

僕人：好的，夫人。

（僕人下。）

馬克白夫人：一切皆非我們所有，全都消耗殆盡，我們擁有欲望，卻絲毫不顯滿足。（馬克白上。）陛下！何以神情如此悲傷？無法改變的事實就應該加以遺忘；事情做了就有如覆水難收。

馬克白：我們刺傷了蛇，卻未能殺死牠；牠會自行療癒，然後我們就置身於危險境地了。還是死了才能得到心靈平靜，毋需再終日提心吊膽。鄧肯已入為安，歷經人世的起伏變動之後，他如今睡得很安穩。我們的背叛已施予他最狠毒的傷害，再也無人能加害於他了。

馬克白夫人：來吧，我的好夫君，整理好你的儀容裝扮，今晚在賓客面前要保持光鮮愉快。

馬克白：親愛的，朕會的，希望夫人亦如是。你要多給班珂一些關注，用眼神和言語向他展現崇敬，因此刻我們暫且還不安全，必須用表情遮掩我們的心，善加偽裝。

馬克白夫人：你必須冷靜。

馬克白：喔，吾心有如蛇蠍，親愛的夫人！班珂與佛良斯仍活在世上。

馬克白夫人：但是他們不會永遠活著。

馬克白：這倒是一大安慰，所以要開心。在蝙蝠飛出洞穴進入黑夜之前，有件可怕的事要先做完。

馬克白夫人：陛下所指是為何事？

馬克白：此事你不宜知曉，屆時再來為我喝采。來吧，黑夜！遮住可悲白晝的溫柔眼睛，用你沾染血腥的隱形毒手，碎裂那使我驚恐至面色蒼白的絆腳石！天光逐漸朦朧，烏鴉亦振翅飛回樹林；白晝的好事開始變得凋零呆滯，而活躍於黑夜掠奪者紛紛出來狩獵。朕之所言令你感到詫異，然而你將見識邪惡如何讓壞事變得更可怕。所以，請你隨朕走一趟。

（兩人下。）

●第三場 ────────────────── P. 060

（皇宮附近的一座花園；三名殺手上。）

殺手一：是何人要你加入我們？

殺手三：馬克白。

殺手二（對殺手一）：我們毫無理由不信任他，畢竟我們是聽命於他。

殺手一：那就與我們同行吧。西方的天空仍有殘存的餘光，晚歸的旅人正快馬加鞭地在入夜前尋覓宿處，我們等待的目標即將接近。

殺手三：聽啊！我聽見馬蹄聲。

班珂（在舞台後面）：給我們一點亮光吧！

殺手二：那人想必就是班珂，晚宴的其餘賓客皆已移駕至庭院。

殺手一：馬夫正要將馬牽回馬廄中，班珂與佛良斯將步行前往皇宮的大門口。

殺手二：我看到亮光了！有亮光！

殺手三：他們即將抵達此地！快準備！

（班珂與佛良斯上；佛良斯手持一把火炬。）

班珂：看來今晚會下雨。

殺手一：就讓大雨傾盆吧！

（殺手一滅了火炬，其他人攻擊班珂。）

班珂：喔，叛逆！跑啊，我的好佛良斯！快跑，快跑，快跑啊！他日要為我報仇！永別了！

（班珂死去；佛良斯逃跑。）

殺手三：是誰滅了火炬？

殺手一：那不是最好的方法嗎？

殺手三：只死了一個，兒子逃跑了。

殺手二：我們的任務中最重要的一部分未能達成！

殺手一：我們必須去稟告馬克白。

（全體下。）

（皇宮內的宴會廳；馬克白、馬克白夫人、羅斯、雷諾克斯、眾領主與侍從們上。）

馬克白：歡迎！爾等之位階各有高低，請就定適合的座位吧。

眾領主：謝謝陛下。

馬克白：朕要和諸位賓客交際一番，扮演好謙遜的主人。女主人會適時地接待各位。

馬克白夫人：請代我說一聲，陛下。告訴我們所有的朋友，我在此衷心歡迎他們。

馬克白（對馬克白夫人）：你瞧——各位賓客都誠摯地感謝你。（對賓客們：）桌席兩側坐的人一般多，朕就坐在中間吧。（殺手一上，站在門口附近。）各位慢慢享用，我們很快就要敬酒準備開席了。（馬克白在賓客們談天之際走向門口，他對殺手一低聲說話。）你臉上有血跡。

殺手一：那就是班珂的血了。

馬克白：沾在你身上好過在他的體內流動。他死了嗎？

殺手一：陛下，他被割了喉嚨，是我親手所為。

馬克白：你割喉的技術堪稱一絕。是誰殺死了佛良斯？倘若是你所為，那你必定是箇中的佼佼者。

殺手一：回稟陛下，佛良斯逃跑了。

馬克白：喔，不！太可怕了！朕的人生原本得以完美，宛如流動的空氣一般自由奔放，然而如今朕被囚禁，被疑慮和恐懼束縛住了。但是，班珂已死？

殺手一：是的，陛下，他陳屍在陰溝裡，頭上有二十道傷口，任何一道傷口都能致他於死地。

馬克白：萬分感謝。成年的毒蛇已死，逃過一劫的小蛇未幾即能生出毒液——然而他未生牙齒。退下吧，此事明日再談。

（殺手一下。）

馬克白夫人：陛下尚未向賓客們敬酒！少了儀式就不成筵席。單純的用餐在家中進行即可，離了家就需要有儀式才能為餐點加味。缺少儀式，筵席就顯得寒酸。請陛下善盡主人之誼，使賓客們感覺賓至如歸吧。

馬克白：多謝夫人的提醒！現在，祝各位身體健康！請享用餐點吧。

雷諾克斯：國王陛下也請入座。

（班珂的鬼魂上，只有馬克白看得見，他坐在馬克白的座位上，但是馬克白尚未看見他。）

馬克白：國內的所有貴族此刻正齊聚一堂，只可惜班珂未能出席。希望他是一時疏忽，而非發生了意外不克前來。

羅斯：他未能履行承諾出席宴會。是否請陛下先入座？

馬克白：已是座無虛席。

雷諾克斯：這兒有個空位，陛下。

馬克白：在哪兒？

雷諾克斯：就在這兒啊，陛下。（雷諾克斯看到馬克白神情慌張；馬克白剛注意到班珂的鬼魂。）怎麼了，陛下？

馬克白：這是誰幹的？

眾領主：陛下所指何事？

馬克白（對鬼魂）：你不能說是朕下的毒手！莫在朕面前甩動你染血的頭髮。

羅斯：各位請起身離席，陛下身體不適。

馬克白夫人：坐吧，諸位好友們，陛下經常如此，他從年輕時就不時會這樣。請回座吧，此乃一時之症狀，未幾即可恢復正常。倘若各位盯著他看，他會被觸怒而使得情況加劇。開動吧，別去注意他。（**對馬克白竊語：**）你是個男人嗎？

馬克白：是的，而且是個膽大的男人，膽敢直視可能嚇壞撒旦之人事物。

馬克白夫人（**對馬克白竊語**）：一派胡言！你在害怕什麼？真是可恥！何以露出此種表情？到頭來，你只是盯著一張空椅子。

馬克白：不，看見沒？你看！看啊！你沒看見嗎？（**對鬼魂：**）哎呀，朕又何必在乎？倘若你不能點頭，想必也無法言語。我們的墳墓非得將下葬之人送回來嗎？或許我們應該將亡者扔去餵鳥。

（**鬼魂消失。**）

馬克白夫人（**對馬克白竊語**）：可恥！

馬克白：我方才站在這兒卻看見了他。在此之前已然濺血；是的，早已有人被殺害，死狀令人不忍聽聞。過去，當大腦受到重創之時，人即會死去，一切就此結束，但是如今亡者又死而復生，將我們從椅凳上推倒；實乃比謀殺血案更奇怪啊！

馬克白夫人：陛下，貴族好友們都在等著你。

馬克白：喔！朕差點忘了。各位貴族好友們，切莫對朕感到詫異；朕生了一種奇怪的病症，但凡熟識朕之人必不覺驚愕。來吧，祝各位身體安康！給朕斟滿整杯的酒吧，朕要向在座諸位敬酒，也敬我們摯愛的好友班珂，他今日不克出席，讓我們舉杯祝賀所有的人和他！

眾領主：祝賀大家！

（鬼魂再上。）

馬克白（對鬼魂）：遠離朕的視線！讓大地藏起你的身影！你的骨骸已成空心，你的血液已然冷卻，你瞠視朕的眼神亦是空洞！

馬克白夫人：各位閣下，就當這只是不幸的病症吧，如此而已，切莫壞了眼前的歡樂氣氛。

馬克白（對鬼魂）：別人敢做之事朕亦敢做，不論你化身為粗暴的俄羅斯熊、披甲的犀牛或張牙舞爪的猛虎！但凡不是你現在的模樣，就必定不能撼動朕的神經。不然重新活過來吧，拔劍單挑朕以一決高下；倘若朕稍有顫抖，就嘲笑朕是個怯懦的小丫頭吧。走開，可怕的幽靈！（鬼魂消失。）哎呀，消失了，朕又能恢復正常了。各位，請回座。

馬克白夫人：陛下的言行失當，不僅壞了眾人的興致，也毀了整場晚宴！

馬克白：發生了此般怪事，如同夏日的雲朵一般突然使朕軟弱，豈不使人詫異？是你讓朕變得對自己陌生，因你看著方才的景象，雙頰卻仍然一如往常地紅潤，然而朕的面容卻因恐懼而蒼白。

羅斯：是何景象，陛下？

馬克白夫人：請你莫再與他交談，他的情況愈來愈糟，質問只會觸怒他。所以，道聲晚安吧。切莫推先讓後地離開，所有的人同時走吧。

雷諾克斯：晚安，願陛下早日康復！

馬克白夫人：大家都晚安吧！

（眾領主與侍從們下。）

馬克白：那個鬼魂想要復仇，朕知道，血債亦須以血償還。現在是何時辰？

馬克白夫人：時已將近午夜。

馬克白：麥德夫並未出席加冕大典，亦忽視了今晚的宴會，夫人作何看法？

馬克白夫人：他有派人來送信嗎？

馬克白：沒有，但是朕明日會派人去送信給他。朕在每位貴族家裡的僕人當中，至少都安排了一名細作，因此麥德夫所言朕都知道得一清二楚。明日朕會去探訪那幾名女巫，因朕此刻不擇手段也決心知道最可怕的消息，此乃為了朕一己私利，其他諸事皆可暫時擱置。朕現已雙腳浸入鮮血之中；倘若血流成河，朕亦須渡河而過。事已至此，往前走會比涉水回頭更容易。朕的腦海裡有奇怪的念頭，不得不付諸實際行動。

馬克白夫人：陛下需要安歇了。

馬克白：來吧，我們去睡了。朕看到鬼魂的怪異景象，乃是初嘗邪惡陰謀者之恐懼。我們畢竟是經驗尚淺啊。

（他們下。）

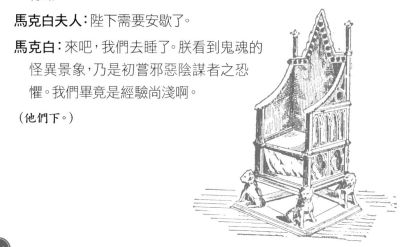

（雷諾克斯與另一位領主上，走進皇宮內的一個房間。）

雷諾克斯：怪事接二連三地發生。先王鄧肯前去探訪馬克白，未幾即遭殺害，接著英勇的班珂深夜外出散步，其子佛良斯亦手刃父親而後逃之夭夭──至少馬克白是如此說服我們相信的。吾人不禁思忖，馬爾康和道南班殺死他們仁慈的父王是何其殘忍之事？簡直太可怕了！馬克白想必悲傷得不能自己！他不是在盛怒之下殺了那兩名守衛嗎？任誰都能看出他們是爛醉如泥而陷入熟睡中，馬克白此舉莫不值得讚賞？是的，而且是明智之舉──因為任誰聽見守衛們矢口否認都會忿恨不平。不知鄧肯的兩個兒子和佛良斯若是落入馬克白手中，他會如何處置他們；相信他們未幾即會因弒父而受到懲罰。但是，我不再多說了！聽聞麥德夫亦是活在恥辱之中，因他不克出席暴君的宴席。閣下，請告知麥德夫目前身在何處？

領主：鄧肯之子馬爾康，亦即遭到馬克白篡奪王位之人，目前正在英格蘭國王愛德華的宮廷中；麥德夫亦已前往英格蘭，協助舉兵攻打馬克白，因馬克白有意與英格蘭交戰。倘若馬爾康與麥德夫皆能大戰告捷，我們有朝一日亦可重獲和平，無需懼怕在宴席之間遭到利刃封喉。

雷諾克斯：但願能有神聖的天使飛入英格蘭宮廷援助麥德夫，祈求我們這蒙受苦難的國家未幾即可回復平靜！

領主：我會為他禱告。

（兩人下。）

第四幕

●第一場 ——————————————— P. 075

（一個黑暗的洞穴，中間有個滾沸的大鍋；雷聲大作；三名女巫上。）

女巫一：圍繞鍋釜轉圈圈，材料投入釜中間。

全體：加快速度，不辭勞苦，熊熊火焰燒著滾沸的鍋釜。

女巫二：此蛇捕於沼澤間，入鍋煮至極沸點。蠑螈的眼睛、青蛙的趾頭，蝙蝠的毛皮、狗兒的舌頭。施以最可怕的魔咒，用邪惡滾沸至濃稠。

全體：加快速度，不辭勞苦，熊熊火焰燒著滾沸的鍋釜。

女巫三：狼的牙齒和龍的鱗片，女巫乾屍的眼睛和指甲片。先加一點、再加許多，悉數投入鍋釜中。

全體：加快速度，不辭勞苦，熊熊火焰燒著滾沸的鍋釜。

女巫二：冷卻之以狒狒血，此咒施下才保險。

女巫三：拇指刺痛使我知，邪惡之事向此至；打開啊，門鎖，不知叩門者為何人！

（馬克白上。）

馬克白：你們幾個行蹤隱密、藏身黑夜的老太婆！這究竟怎麼回事？

全體：一件不知名的事。

馬克白：朕有幾個問題想請教。

女巫一：問我們或我們的主人？

馬克白：喚來他們，讓朕親眼得見。

女巫一：倒進母豬的鮮血，牠吃了親生的九隻仔豬。還有從絞刑架上取來的汗水，全都投入火堆。

全體：來吧，不管高低出身，在我們面前快快現身！

（雷聲大作；幻影一，戴著甲冑的一個頭，從大鍋中浮現出來。）

幻影一：馬克白！馬克白！馬克白！提防麥德夫，注意伐夫領主。
我走了，我言盡於此。

（幻影一消失在大鍋中。）

女巫一：他將不會再出現，再來還有比上一個更強的先知。

（雷聲大作；幻影二，一個滿身是血的嬰孩，從大鍋中浮現出來。）

幻影二：要強硬、大膽而堅決，用大笑去輕蔑凡人的力量，因
為沒有任何女人所生者能傷害得了馬克白！

（幻影二消失在大鍋中。）

馬克白：你就活著吧，麥德夫！朕又何須懼怕你？然而朕還是
要再三確定，擔保朕的命運——不能留你活口，好讓朕不
再心生恐懼，即便雷聲隆隆也得以安眠。

（雷聲大作；幻影三，一個頭戴王冠、手裡拿著樹的嬰孩，從大鍋中浮
現出來。）

馬克白：這是什麼？何以看似國王之子，初生的額頭上戴著象
徵權位的王冠？

全體：仔細聽，但切莫與之交談。

幻影三：要英勇如獅子，得意自豪，切莫擔憂你的敵人們。馬
克白永遠不敗，除非伯南樹林移到當希南山與之為敵。

（幻影三消失在大鍋中。）

馬克白：此事決不可能發生！何人能迫使樹林去與人交戰？真
好的預言，好極了！伯南樹林未移動，叛軍亦無法行動，馬
克白國王將會長命百歲。然而有個事實仍使朕不寒而慄：告
訴朕，班珂的兒子們是否終將統治這個王國。

全體：切莫再追問。

馬克白：朕必須知道！倘若你們拒絕，將會受到永恆的詛咒！
告訴朕——

全體：讓他親眼得見，使他內心悲痛。來無影，去亦無蹤！

（八位國王與班珂出現，後者手持一面鏡子從大鍋中浮現出來。）

馬克白（輪流對每位國王說）：你的長相未免也太像班珂的亡
魂了！快下去！你的王冠使朕的眼睛刺痛！你的頭髮金碧輝
煌，如同前者一般。第三個也同於其餘幾個。醜陋的老太婆
們！何以令朕目睹此景？還有第四個！怎麼？這個隊伍沒完
沒了嗎？竟然還有！第七個！朕不想再看下去了！然而又出
現第八個，手持一面鏡子使朕又看到更多。可怕的景象啊！
如今朕親眼所見，此乃為真，他們都將成為國王！已然濺血
的班珂衝著朕微笑，手指著他們，彷彿在說他們皆為他的
子孫。什麼！果真如此嗎？

女巫一：是的，陛下，此情此景乃是事實。但是馬克白何以如
此驚愕地站在這兒？來吧，姐妹們，我們先行告退。我將施
咒使空氣出聲，你們則在此舞動其身，好讓這位國王心滿
意足，因其疑問我們皆已答覆。

（音樂；女巫們跳舞，然後消失。）

馬克白：她們去了哪裡？不見了？讓這邪惡的時刻得到詛咒！
朕聽見有腳步聲，進來吧，不論來者何人！

（雷諾克斯上。）

雷諾克斯：陛下有何吩咐？

馬克白：你是否看見那些怪異的姐妹們？

雷諾克斯：回稟陛下，沒有。

馬克白：她們並未與你擦身而過？

雷諾克斯：回稟陛下，確實沒有。

馬克白：朕聽見馬蹄聲，是何人來此？

雷諾克斯：屬下幾人前來稟告陛下，麥德夫已逃往英格蘭。

馬克白：逃往英格蘭！

雷諾克斯：回稟陛下，是的。

馬克白（竊語）：倘若朕未曾來此，或許仍有時間攔下麥德夫。從今爾後朕將劍及履及。朕將奇襲麥德夫的城堡，以利刃殺死他的妻子、孩子們，和恰巧在場的所有不幸的親戚們。朕不會傻到四處吹噓此事，只會在怒氣消去之前完成此舉。

（對雷諾克斯：）這幾位紳士身在何處？來吧，領朕前去會會他們。

（全體下。）

（伐夫，麥德夫城堡內的一個房間；麥德夫夫人、她的兒子與羅斯上。）

麥德夫夫人：他犯了何事被迫離開蘇格蘭？

羅斯：夫人請務必耐心等待。

麥德夫夫人：他並未犯事，實乃一時衝動才會逃跑，此舉使人疑心他是個叛徒。

羅斯：他是出於深思熟慮或一時恐懼才離開，我們不得而知。

麥德夫夫人：深思熟慮！拋下他的妻子、他的寶貝兒女們、他的城堡和他的頭銜，逃離屬於他的這一切？他對我們已無愛，人性感情皆已泯滅。即使鷦鷯，最微小不起眼的鳥兒，也會為了保護幼子而奮力對抗貓頭鷹，他卻滿心恐懼而無愛，違悖常理地逃命去了。

羅斯：我親愛的表親，請你務必冷靜，你的夫君乃高尚、明智而審慎之人，對當今的問題皆瞭若指掌。我不敢再多言，然而如今時局艱難，竟被人不分青紅皂白地指控為叛徒！我們漂流在波濤洶湧的海上，無論往哪個方向都會被海浪吞噬。請容我先行告辭，但是我未幾即可歸來。願上帝保佑你，我美麗的表親！

（羅斯下。）

麥德夫夫人：吾兒，你父親已死，如今你可怎麼辦？你要如何活下去？

兒子：如同鳥兒一般，母親。

麥德夫夫人：什麼？以蟲子和蒼蠅為食？

兒子：不，我有什麼就吃什麼，如同牠們一般。

麥德夫夫人：可憐的鳥兒！難道你不害怕陷阱、獵人、抑或圈套嗎？

兒子：我又何須害怕，母親？「窮苦的」鳥兒不會被人獵捕。我父親未死，縱使你說他已死。

麥德夫夫人：是的，他死了，你沒了父親該如何？

兒子：不，是你沒了丈夫該如何？

麥德夫夫人：我隨便上市場就能買二十個。

兒子：那你就去買來轉賣吧。

麥德夫夫人：你講的只是童言童語！

兒子：我父親是個叛徒嗎，母親？

麥德夫夫人：是的，他是。

兒子：何謂叛徒？

麥德夫夫人：滿口粗話和謊言之人。

兒子：但凡叛徒皆如此嗎？

麥德夫夫人：凡如是者皆為叛徒，都要被絞死。

兒子：滿口粗話和謊言之人都要被絞死？

麥德夫夫人：無一例外。

兒子：要由誰來絞死他們？

麥德夫夫人：當然是誠實之人。

兒子：那滿口謊言和粗話之人都是傻瓜，因為如是之人多到足以打倒誠實之人，將他們悉數絞死。

麥德夫夫人：願上帝保佑你，可憐的頑皮孩子！但是你沒了父親該如何？

兒子：倘若他已死，你會為他哭泣；倘若你並未為他哭泣，此乃一好兆頭，意味著我未幾將會有個新父親。

麥德夫夫人：你講這什麼話！

（一名信差上。）

信差：祝福你，美麗的夫人！你不認識我，但是我知道你是何人。請你務必離開此地，快帶著孩子們逃跑吧！此處有人處心積慮意圖傷害你，願上帝助你！我亦不敢久留此地。

（信差下。）

麥德夫夫人：要我逃去哪兒？我未曾犯下傷人之事，但是我如今想起自己乃身在俗世間，經常傷人才是值得嘉許之事，行善反而是可能招禍之愚行。哎呀，那我又何必表露婦人之見，說我未曾傷人來防禦自己？（殺手們上。）來者何人？

殺手一：你的夫君何在？

麥德夫夫人：希望他並未置身於此般危險之境地，讓你們這些人找到他。

殺手一：他是個叛徒。

兒子：滿口謊言，你這蓬髮的惡徒！

殺手一（刺死他）：你這黃口小兒！你是叛徒之子！

兒子：他殺了我，母親。快逃跑吧，我懇求你！

（兒子死去；麥德夫夫人下，大喊著「殺人！」殺手們隨她下。）

（英格蘭，在國王的皇宮前面；馬爾康與麥德夫上。）

馬爾康：讓我們找個僻靜的陰暗處，在那兒哭泣直到我們把眼淚都流乾。

麥德夫：讓我們拾起劍，前往我們那已滅亡的國家。每天早上都有新寡的婦人在嚎啕，都有新的孤兒在啼哭，天堂都因為新的哀傷而難過；天堂回應了蘇格蘭的苦難，喊出相同哀悼的字句。

馬爾康：我會為了發生之事而哭泣，但是我能改變的就會去改變。你或許所言為真，你曾愛戴這位暴君，如今說出他的名字卻令我們舌頭生膿瘡。他至今尚未動你半根汗毛，使我不禁疑心你可能仍然效忠於他。又或許你是打算背叛我以博取他的寵信──可憐又無辜的羔羊──藉此平息神的憤怒。

麥德夫：我並無叛逆之意！

馬爾康：但是馬克白有，即使天性良善又有美德之人，也可能聽從國王的命令而有卑鄙之舉。然而要請求你原諒我有此般的想法，畢竟你的本性並非我的念頭所能改變。

麥德夫：我已失去了希望。

馬爾康：我原本不解你為何拋下妻兒，對你的至愛不告而別。然而，我仍然沒理由不信任你。不論我的擔憂為何，你都是正直而忠實之人。

麥德夫：淌血啊，它在淌血啊，可憐的國家！殘虐的暴政！再會了，殿下，不論那個暴君賜與任何土地予我，我都不會成為你所疑心的不忠之徒！

馬爾康：切莫動怒，我並未真心疑懼你的赤誠之心。我國在馬克白的統治之下民不聊生，每天都有新傷加在舊痕之上，我想應該會有很多人擁戴我；事實上，英格蘭國王已派遣數千大軍前來支援我。但是儘管有大軍增援，待他日我踩在那個暴君頭上而過，或是用我的劍抹了他的脖子之時，我可憐的國家還是會有比從前更多舛的命運，而且在很多方面，在馬克白之後的繼任者可能會給人民帶來更多苦難。

麥德夫：那繼任者會是何人？

馬爾康：我指的是我自己。我深知自身的缺點何在，待他人看透我的缺點，即使邪惡的馬克白也會顯得潔白似雪。相較於我將帶來的無盡傷害，全國人民會視他為羔羊。

麥德夫：說到邪惡，馬克白是無可比擬的！

馬爾康：我認同他是殘暴、好色、貪婪、虛偽、欺詐和暴戾，舉凡世間所有的罪皆與他沾上邊。然而我的邪惡可是毫無底限──完全沒有。即使你的妻妾們、女兒們、侍女們、甚至家中的老婦人們，也都無法滿足我的感官肉慾。讓馬克白統治也好，總好過如我這般的人即位吧。

麥德夫：如此之肉慾並非天生，應為極大的不快樂和許多國王的覆滅所致。但是切莫畏於取回屬於你應得之物，屆時會有許多女人樂意隨身服侍你。

馬爾康：那並非我唯一的缺陷；我亦是貪婪之人，倘若由我繼位為王，我會取走所有貴族們的土地，下令這個進貢珠寶首飾、那個獻上豪宅房屋，我得到的愈多就會更慾望無窮，直至最後與良善忠誠之士發生不當的口角衝突，為了財富而毀滅他們。

麥德夫：此般貪婪比起年少的肉慾更顯可怕，這是奪去許多國王性命的劍。但是你切莫驚恐，蘇格蘭有數不盡的財富能滿足你，不會傷害任何人；你的缺點皆可被容忍，還是想想你的美德吧。

馬爾康：無奈我毫無美德。身為國王應有的品德——公正、誠實、節制中庸、情緒穩定、慷慨、慈悲、謙恭、奉獻、耐心、勇氣——在我身上無一可見。反之，我傾向於犯罪，在許多方面都顯露無遺。不，倘若是我掌權，我會擾亂全天下的平靜，混亂世上所有的統一局面。

麥德夫：喔，蘇格蘭啊，蘇格蘭！

馬爾康：倘若此等人適合居於王位，請明說；我是真如我方才所言這般啊。

麥德夫：適合居於王位？不，連活著都不配！喔，不幸的國家！在位者是個殘忍嗜血的暴君，倘若正統的繼位者不適合居於王位，何時能重現和平的曙光？馬爾康，你的父王鄧肯是最崇高的國王，誕下你的王后母親亦是每日禱告過著虔誠的生活。再會了！你自白的這些邪惡之事，將使我永世不再踏進蘇格蘭半步。喔，我的國家！你的希望終結於此！

馬爾康：麥德夫，你對蘇格蘭的崇高熱愛讓我明白了你的榮譽之心，亦向我證明了你是值得信任的。邪惡的馬克白經常賜與女人、權力和財富予我，意圖收買我效忠於他——然而你並未如此。現在我要向你坦承我方才所言之缺失皆非事實，我未曾與女人同床共枕，亦未曾有半句虛言，甚至未曾覬覦理應屬於我的一切。我未曾違悖自己的信仰，亦未曾背叛過任何人。我對事實一如對生命一般地珍視，此生第一個謊言即是對你細數我的邪惡之處。真正的我實乃如是：
對你和對我可憐的國家，我隨時聽候差遣；我一心只想好好
報效我的國家。事實上，在你來到此地之前，一位英格蘭將
領帶著萬名英勇的士兵，準備前往蘇格蘭背水一戰。你我
同往吧！但是你何以緘口不言？

麥德夫：同時聽聞如此的好消息和壞消息！一時之間難以概括
承受。你瞧，來者何人？

馬爾康：我不認得他。

（羅斯上。）

麥德夫：高尚的表親，歡迎來到英格蘭。

馬爾康：現在我知道他是何人了！我離開蘇格蘭時日已久，但
願這一切未幾即可結束！

羅斯：殿下，但願如此。

麥德夫：蘇格蘭是否仍一如往昔？

羅斯：哎呀，可憐的國家——幾乎不敢看清自己的模樣了！如
今不能說是我們的母國，而是成了我們的墳墓。隨處可聞嘆
息、哀嚎和尖叫聲，暴力與悲悽無所不在。經常聞得喪鐘響
起，也沒人多問死者是何人。在盛開後的花朵凋零之前，好
人的生命即已逝去，甚至未有臥病在床的機會就死去了。

馬爾康：最新令人悲痛之事為何？

羅斯：一小時前發生的事即已成為舊聞，每一分鐘都有新的事
件發生。

麥德夫：我的夫人還好嗎？

羅斯：那當然，依然平靜地健在。

麥德夫：那我的孩子們呢？

羅斯：在我告別他們時依然很好。

麥德夫：切莫吝嗇地語帶保留！蘇格蘭目前的情勢究竟為何？

羅斯：聽聞許多蘇格蘭貴族已興兵反抗暴君，我相信此傳言為真，因我親眼目睹暴君的士兵們行軍赴戰。如今我們需要支援。（對馬爾康：）可惜你未能身在蘇格蘭，否則士兵們必會追隨你，即使女人也會為了除去馬克白而親上戰場。

馬爾康：知會他們，我們會儘快趕到。英格蘭國王已派遣優秀的西華德，調借萬名大軍準備前來相助；他是久經沙場的傑出軍人，踏破鐵鞋亦難覓得。

羅斯：但願我也能回敬以好消息，無奈我要說的話只應在沙漠中呼喊，免得被任何人聽見。

麥德夫：你要說的是什麼話？是舉國同哀之事？抑或是單一個人的悲傷之事？

羅斯：但凡誠實之人聽到這些話皆會同悲，唯主要是與你一人有關。

麥德夫：倘若真與我有關，就請你務必告訴我。快，告訴我吧！

羅斯：切莫讓你的耳朵怨恨我的舌頭，因我將親口說出在你聽來最沉重的話語。

麥德夫：我大概猜得到你要說的是什麼。

羅斯：你的城堡被人突襲，你的夫人和幼子們皆慘遭殺害。我無法再多告知細節，否則我恐怕你會承受不住。

馬爾康：慈悲的上帝！麥德夫，將你的悲傷化為言語吧！將悲傷壓抑在心中只會更加地悲痛欲絕。

麥德夫：我的孩子們也遇害了？

羅斯：妻子、孩子們、僕人們——無一倖免。

麥德夫：而我竟然拋下他們！我的夫人也遇害了？

羅斯：我方才已經說過。

馬爾康：請你節哀順變，讓我們用復仇來療癒這深切的哀痛。

麥德夫：但是馬克白膝下無子啊。我所有可愛的孩子們？你說他們全死了？無一倖免？我可愛的孩子們和他們的母親，全被一舉屠殺？

馬爾康：你要像個男子漢一般前去復仇。

麥德夫：我也要像個男子漢一般去感受。我情不自禁地想起那些我最珍愛的親人們，難道老天就這麼袖手旁觀而不予以援助嗎？他們皆是因我而死——不是因為他們犯了錯，而是因為我的過失。但願他們此刻得以安息！

馬爾康：用這份哀痛來磨利你的劍，化悲憤為力量。你的心切莫遲鈍——要激怒它！

麥德夫：慈悲的上帝，莫再蹉跎，即刻帶我去面對這個蘇格蘭暴君，用我的劍挑戰他；他若膽敢逃跑，就讓老天寬恕他吧！

馬爾康：有這個念頭就對了！來，我們去找國王。大軍已蓄勢待發，一聲令下即可出兵。眼看馬克白就要像樹上成熟的果子一般落地了，等著被推翻。你要振作精神，否則難以熬過這漫漫長夜。

（全體下。）

第五幕

●第一場―――――――――――――――――――――――― P. 099

（當希南，在城堡內的一個房間；一位醫生與一位仕女上。）

仕女： 自從國王陛下領軍出征後，我已見她這樣做過許多次。她從床上起身，取出一張紙、折疊、在上頭寫字，然後念出來，接著封緘，再躺回床上。這一切皆在她熟睡的狀態下進行。

醫生： 她有說過什麼嗎？

仕女： 她說了很多，醫生，我還是別告訴你比較好。

醫生： 你可以告訴我。事實上，你應該告訴我。

仕女： 不，我沒有證人可為我佐證。你瞧――她來了！（馬克白夫人上，手持一根蠟燭。）她就是這副模樣。你看，她正在熟睡的狀態。仔細看好，站過去一點。

醫生： 她手裡的蠟燭是哪兒來的？

仕女： 這是她的吩咐，她睡前都要在床畔點上蠟燭。

醫生： 你瞧，她的雙眼是睜開的！

仕女： 是的，但她是視而不見。

醫生： 仔細看她在搓揉雙手！

仕女： 是的，她看似在洗手，我有一回看她這樣做了十五分鐘。

馬克白夫人： 手上仍然有污點。

醫生： 你聽，她說話了！我來寫下她說了些什麼，好作個記錄。

馬克白夫人：去掉吧，該死的污點！我叫你去掉！一點鐘、兩點鐘。哎呀，下手的時辰到了。夫君，切莫擔心有誰會知曉，因我們現在的權力已是至高無上。但是誰又料想得到那老頭身上的血會那麼多？

醫生：你聽見了嗎？

馬克白夫人：伐夫領主曾經有位夫人，此刻她身在何處？怎麼這雙手永遠洗不乾淨？別再這樣了，夫君，適可而止吧，你再這樣有如驚弓之鳥就會毀了一切。

醫生（對馬克白夫人）：你似乎得知了你不該知道的事。

馬克白夫人（用手摸鼻子）：這裡還是有血腥味。（嘆息：）用盡阿拉伯的所有香水也無法使這隻小手變香。

醫生：如此悲痛的呻吟！她的心頭沉重。

仕女：不論用什麼來交換，我也不要這樣的一顆心！

醫生：此病已非我所能診治。

馬克白夫人：洗淨你的雙手，切莫如此神色蒼白。我告訴你──班珂已經下葬！他不可能再從墳墓裡爬出來了。去睡吧！喔！有人在敲門。來吧，來？把手給我，已經做了的事就如覆水難收。去睡吧，去睡吧，去睡吧。

（馬克白夫人下。）

醫生：她現在要去睡了嗎？

仕女：現在就去。

醫生：我過去亦曾聽人低語自己做過的惡行。她需要上天的伸援──我愛莫能助！好好照顧她。現在，晚安了。我方才之所見令我眼界大開，只能意會，但是我不敢言傳。

（兩人下。）

●第二場

（當希南附近的鄉下；鼓聲響起；曼泰斯、凱瑟尼斯、安格斯、雷諾克斯與士兵們上。）

曼泰斯：英格蘭大軍逼近，由馬爾康、西華德和麥德夫領軍。他們心中燒灼著復仇的烈火，理由充分到即使已死之人也會復活援助他們！

安格斯：我們到伯南樹林附近攔截他們，他們正往那個方向行進。

凱瑟尼斯：道南班是否與他的兄長在一起？

雷諾克斯：想當然爾，閣下，他必定不是。我手上有全體士兵的名單，其中有西華德之子，還有許多嘴上無毛的年輕小伙子，自以為長大了可以上陣殺敵。

曼泰斯：馬克白那個暴君在做什麼？

凱瑟尼斯：在當希南保護他的城堡。有人說他瘋了，也有些沒那麼憎恨他的人稱他的備戰為英勇的憤怒。

安格斯：如今他自覺殺人密行使他的雙手染血無法去除！目前每日皆有小型叛變，挑戰他的王權。他旗下的大軍只因聽命於他而接受他的指揮──而非因為士兵們愛戴他。如今他的頭銜已成了虛名，就好比矮子賊罩上巨人的長袍一般。

凱瑟尼斯：讓我們繼續前行，順服於真正值得效忠之人。我們未幾即可遇見馬爾康，他才是能治癒蘇格蘭和我們眾人的良藥。

雷諾克斯：好，我們繼續前往伯南樹林吧。

（全體行軍下。）

第五幕

第二場

171

● 第三場

（當希南，城堡內的一個房間；馬克白、醫生與侍從們上。）

馬克白：別再向朕報告情況了。除非伯南樹林移到當希南山，否則朕無需心生畏懼。馬爾康算什麼？他不也是女人所生嗎？可預知世事的女巫們是這麼告訴朕的：「沒有任何女人所生者能傷害馬克白。」（一名僕人上。）有什麼事，你這臉色蒼白的呆子？

僕人：有一萬名……

馬克白：呆子嗎，惡徒？

僕人：是士兵，陛下。

馬克白：何以神色如此驚恐，你這個膽小鬼？什麼士兵，傻瓜？

僕人：是英格蘭大軍，陛下。

馬克白：你可以滾出去了！（僕人下。）朕心已疲累。此一戰若非鞏固朕的王位，就是使朕被人推翻。朕活得夠久了，青春年華已逝去，遲暮之年應有之良伴，譬如榮譽、愛、服從、摯友，朕都不指望能擁有了；反之，服從朕之人皆出於畏懼。（對醫生：）病人的情況如何，醫生？

醫生：她的身體無恙，陛下，但是她內心為幻覺所苦而夜夜不得成眠。

馬克白：把她治好。難道你治不好心靈上的疾病，無法拔除根植於記憶中的憂傷，不能抹去刻印在腦海中的煩惱嗎？再用些令人遺忘的解藥，洗淨那壓在她胸口危險重重的包袱！

醫生：照這情況看來，病人得靠自己調養了。

馬克白：把藥扔去餵狗吧！朕不需要了。醫生，領主們皆已背棄朕。倘若你能診斷出這個國家的病根，就設法讓它回復健康吧。

醫生：回稟陛下，我力有未逮。

馬克白：我不會害怕死亡和痛苦，除非伯南樹林移動到當希南。

（全體下，獨留醫生一人。）

醫生：倘若我能逃離當希南，我就自在逍遙了。給我再多的好處我也不可能留在此地。

（醫生下。）

●第四場

（伯南樹林附近的鄉下；鼓聲響起；馬爾康、老西華德及其子、麥德夫、
曼泰斯、安格斯、凱瑟尼斯、雷諾克斯、羅斯與士兵們行軍上。）

西華德：我們眼前這是什麼樹林？

曼泰斯：是伯南樹林。

馬爾康：讓每個士兵都砍下一截枝葉，攜在身前作掩護，如此
即可使敵軍摸不清我們的人數，讓探子回報錯誤的軍情給
馬克白吧。

士兵們：謹遵指示。

西華德：聽聞馬克白仍在當希南，在那兒等著我們的到來。

馬爾康：此乃他的一線曙光，因他知道他的手下在戰場上能比
在城堡內更輕易地背棄他。唯有被強迫之人才效忠於他，
他們的心早已投向他處。

麥德夫：讓我們專心於眼前的戰役吧，好士兵是不會因謠言而
分心的。

西華德：時辰已至，我們將可得知自己能擁有什麼，又會虧欠
什麼。臆測結果只會顯露出我們的期望，而一旦出擊即可分
曉勝負。所以，開戰吧。

（全體行軍下。）

（當希南，城堡內；馬克白、西登與士兵們上。）

馬克白：將我軍之旗幟掛在城牆外邊，讓我們守得固若金湯的城堡去嘲笑他們，讓他們在那兒等著飢餓和發熱而喪命。若非背棄我們的士兵們前去增援，我們恐怕就能與敵軍短兵相接，打得他們回老家去。（屋內傳來淒厲的哭喊聲。）那是什麼聲音？

西登：回稟陛下，是女人的尖叫聲。

（西登下。）

馬克白：朕幾乎忘了恐懼為何物。曾幾何時，朕在夜半聽到尖叫聲就會背脊發涼，驚嚇到汗毛直豎。但如今朕已飽嘗恐怖的滋味，如此可怕的尖叫聲再也無法使朕驚嚇。（西登再上。）方才何以傳來尖叫聲？

西登：回稟陛下，王后死了。

馬克白：她應該晚一點再死——應該等到朕有哀悼的閒暇。明天，和明天，再一個明天，日復一日地躡足緩步前行，直到最後的一分一秒；所有的昨天只是為傻子照亮了通往回歸塵土之路。熄滅，熄滅吧，短暫的燭光！人生只是行走的陰影，在舞台上焦躁踱步的拙劣演員，爾後便乏人問津。這是一個由白癡在敘述的故事，充滿了喧囂和憤怒，毫無意義可言。（一名信差上。）你是來傳遞訊息的，快說吧。

信差：當我站在山頭上守衛之時，我俯瞰著伯南，彷彿感覺樹林開始移動了！

馬克白：倘若你有半句虛言，朕就把你吊在最近的樹上讓你活活餓死。倘若你所言屬實，朕不在乎你是否也對朕如法炮製。朕開始懷疑那幻影是以模稜兩可的謊言在哄騙朕：「馬克白永遠不會被打敗，除非柏南樹林移到當希南。」你說真的有樹林移往當希南嗎？所有士兵全副武裝！準備迎戰！鳴響警報聲！吹吧，狂風！來吧，敵軍！至少我們要馬革裹屍戰死沙場。

（全體下。）

●第六場 ————————————————P. 113

（在城堡前方的一處平原；鼓聲響起；馬爾康、老西華德、麥德夫和他們的軍隊上，以樹木的枝葉掩護。）

馬爾康：我們目前已經夠接近了，扔掉你們的枝葉偽裝，露出原本的面貌吧。（對老西華德：）你，高尚的叔父，要和我的表親、你的貴族兒子一同領軍發動我們的第一波攻擊，再來就由我與英勇的麥德夫接手。

西華德：就此別過。倘若我們今晚遇上那暴君的軍隊，萬一我們無力反抗，就讓我們戰敗吧。

麥德夫：吹響我們所有的號角——給敵軍高聲傳頌鮮血和死亡的氣息。

（全體下。）

（平原上的另一塊地方；馬克白上。）

馬克白：朕有如被綁在木椿上的一頭熊，跑也跑不了，但是又如同熊一般必須奮戰到底。怎麼可能有人不是女人所生？我要懼怕的是這種人──否則我無所畏懼。

（小西華德上。）

小西華德：來者報上名號？

馬克白：朕乃馬克白是也。

小西華德：即使是撒旦報上的名號，在我聽來也不比此名更令人憎恨。

馬克白：是，也不比此名更令人畏懼。

小西華德：你滿口謊言，令人厭惡的暴君！我要用我的劍來證明。

（他們打鬥，小西華德被殺死。）

馬克白：你是女人所生！朕對著劍微笑；但凡女人所生者使用的兵器，朕皆嗤之以鼻。

（馬克白下；小西華特的遺體被抬下舞台；麥德夫上。）

第五幕
第七場

麥德夫：暴君，露臉吧！倘若你被殺死卻非我親手所為，我妻
　　兒的鬼魂會永遠糾纏著我。我不會攻擊你那些不幸的士兵
　　們，他們僅是為了錢而戰鬥。我只會攻擊你，馬克白，否則
　　我寧願收劍回鞘。由這些聲音足以判定，你們應該很接近
　　了。讓我找到他吧，命運之神！我只有這個要求。

（麥德夫下；馬爾康與老西華德上。）

西華德：殿下這邊請，城堡已被包圍，貴族領主們已傳來捷報！
　　我軍未幾即可大獲全勝，僅剩一點細微末節要收尾。

馬爾康：我們從前也遇過臨陣倒戈的敵軍。

西華德：請進城堡吧，殿下。

（全體下。）

（戰場上的另一塊地方；馬克白上。）

馬克白：何以要朕用劍殺死自己，只因我軍節節敗退？朕還看到活著的敵軍，就應該全力殺敵。

（麥德夫上。）

麥德夫：轉過身來，你這惡徒，轉身！

馬克白：在場的所有人當中，朕迴避你已久。回去吧，回去！朕的靈魂已沾染太多你親屬家眷的血跡。

麥德夫：我氣憤到無言以對了──只得用劍洩憤。你這惡徒雙手沾染的鮮血已非我所能言喻！

（他們打鬥。）

馬克白：你是在白費力氣，不如拿劍去對付空氣，別再想方設法要讓我濺血了！讓你的劍刃砍在你傷得了的人身上，我有魔法護身，但凡女人所生者皆傷不了我。

麥德夫：這個魔法失效了！就讓你仍效忠的撒旦來告訴你：麥德夫未足月時就從他母親的子宮被剖出來。我並非以尋常方式所生。

馬克白：詛咒那些告訴朕這些話的人，因朕聞此即勇氣全消！那些騙人的魔鬼全都滿口謊言，他們語帶雙關地哄騙我們。朕不會與你交手。

麥德夫：那就投降吧，懦夫──活下來表演供人觀賞！我們會將你的肖像畫在柱子上，把你當作稀有猛獸一般對待，在底下寫著：「此即暴君的下場。」

馬克白：朕決不投降，決不拜倒在年輕的馬爾康腳下，飽受百姓們的奚落辱罵。所以伯南樹林果真移動到當希南，而你也並非女人所生！但是朕仍要戰到最後，用英勇好戰的盾牌掩護朕的身體。繼續打吧，麥德夫，誰先喊出「夠了！」誰就要受到詛咒。

（他們下，繼續打鬥；鼓聲響起；馬爾康、老西華德、羅斯、雷諾克斯、安格斯、凱瑟尼斯、曼泰斯與士兵們上。）

馬爾康：喔，原來我們缺席的好友們皆已平安抵達此地！

西華德：戰場上必有人喪命；但是，看來我軍的死傷並不多。

馬爾康：麥德夫不見人影，還有令郎也是。

羅斯：閣下，令郎已戰死沙場。他甫成年即已夭折，然而他是像個男子漢一般死在戰場上。

西華德：你說他死了？

僕人：是的，切莫因他的價值而哀傷過度，否則你的悲憤將會綿綿無絕期。

西華德：他的致命傷是在正面嗎？

羅斯：是的，在他身體的正面。

西華德：那就表示他是英勇戰死的，面對著他的敵人。縱使我有如頭髮一般多的兒子，我亦不敢奢求他們各個皆能如他一般死得重如泰山。所以，願上帝與他同在。

（麥德夫上，提著馬克白的首級。）

麥德夫（對馬爾康）：為國王歡呼！你們看，此乃暴君被詛咒的頭顱。我們重獲自由了，蘇格蘭國王萬歲！

全體：蘇格蘭國王萬歲！

（號角聲響起。）

馬爾康：朕將不會有任何耽擱，馬上就會嘉獎各位今日的英勇表現。各位領主和親友們，從今爾後汝等即被加封為伯爵，蘇格蘭第一批受此封銜之人。吾等未幾將召喚流亡在外的朋友們返鄉，並讓效忠於這已死之殺人魔頭及其惡毒王后的殘酷臣子們悉數接受審判；據說那女魔頭已然自我了斷。所以要感謝諸位，也邀請你們前往斯康出席加冕大典。

（號角聲響起；全體下。）

Literary Glossary ● 文學詞彙表

aside 竊語

一種台詞。演員在台上講此台詞時,其他角色是聽不見的。角色通常藉由竊語來向觀眾抒發內心感受。

■ Although she appeared to be calm, the heroine's **aside** revealed her inner terror.
雖然女主角看似冷靜,但她的**竊語**透露出她內在的恐懼。

backstage 後台

一個戲院空間。演員都在此處準備上台,舞台布景也存放此處。

■ Before entering, the villain impatiently waited **backstage**.
在上台前,壞人在**後台**焦躁地等待。

cast 演員;卡司陣容

戲劇的全體演出人員。

■ The entire **cast** must attend tonight's dress rehearsal.
全體演員必須參加今晚的正式排練。

character 角色

故事或戲劇中虛構的人物。

■ Mighty Mouse is one of my favorite cartoon **characters**.
太空飛鼠是我最愛的卡通**人物**之一。

climax 劇情高峰

戲劇或小說中主要衝突的結局。

■ The outlaw's capture made an exciting **climax** to the story.
逃犯落網成為故事中最刺激的**精彩情節**。

comedy 喜劇

有趣好笑的戲劇、電影和電視劇，並有快樂完美的結局。

- My friends and I always enjoy a Jim Carrey **comedy**.
  我朋友和我總是很喜歡金凱瑞演的**喜劇**。

conflict 戲劇衝突

故事主要的角色較量、勢力對抗或想法衝突。

- *Dr. Jekyll and Mr. Hyde* illustrates the **conflict** between good and evil.
  《變身怪醫》描述善惡之間的**衝突**。

conclusion 尾聲

解決情節衝突的方法，使故事結束。

- That play's **conclusion** was very satisfying. Every conflict was resolved. 該劇的**結局**十分令人滿意，所有的衝突都被圓滿解決。

dialogue 對白

小說或戲劇角色所說的話語。

- Amusing **dialogue** is an important element of most comedies.
  有趣的**對白**是大多喜劇中重要的元素之一。

drama 戲劇

故事，通常非喜劇類型，特別是寫來讓演員在戲劇或電影中演出。

- The TV **drama** about spies was very suspenseful.
  那齣關於間諜的電視**劇**非常懸疑。

event 事件

發生的事情；特別的事。

- The most exciting **event** in the story was the surprise ending.
  故事中最精彩的**事件**是意外的結局。

introduction 簡介

一篇簡短的文章，呈現並解釋小說或戲劇的劇情。

- The **introduction** to *Frankenstein* is in the form of a letter.
  《科學怪人》的**簡介**是以信件的型式呈現。

motive 動機

一股內在或外在的力量，迫使角色做出某些事情。

- What was that character's **motive** for telling a lie?
  那個角色說謊的**動機**為何？

passage 段落

書寫作品的部分內容，範圍短至一行，長至幾段。

- His favorite **passage** from the book described the author's childhood.
  他在書中最喜歡的**段落**描述了該作者的童年。

playwright 劇作家

戲劇的作者。

- William Shakespeare is the world's most famous **playwright**.
  威廉莎士比亞是世界上最知名的**劇作家**。

plot 情節

故事或戲劇中一連串的因果事件，導致最終結局。

- The **plot** of that mystery story is filled with action.
  該推理故事的**情節**充滿打鬥。

point of view 觀點

由角色的心理層面來看待故事發展的狀況。

- The father's **point of view** about elopement was quite different from the daughter's. 父親對於私奔的**看法**與女兒迥然不同。

prologue 序幕

在戲劇第一幕開始前的介紹。

- The **playwright** described the main characters in the **prologue** to the play.

  劇作家在**序幕**中描述了主要角色。

quotation 名句

被引述的文句；某角色所說的詞語；在引號內的文字。

- A popular **quotation** from *Julius Caesar* begins, "Friends, Romans, countrymen . . ."

  《凱薩大帝》中**常被引用的文句**開頭是：「各位朋友，各位羅馬人，各位同胞……」。

role 角色

演員在劇中揣摩表演的人物。

- Who would you like to see play the **role** of Romeo?

  你想看誰飾演羅密歐這個**角色**呢？

sequence 順序

故事或事件發生的時序。

- Sometimes actors rehearse their scenes out of **sequence**.

  演員有時會不按**順序**排練他們出場的戲。

setting 情節背景

故事發生的地點與時間。

- This play's **setting** is New York in the 1940s.

  戲劇的**背景設定**於 1940 年代的紐約。

soliloquy 獨白

角色向觀眾發表想法的一番言論，猶如自言自語。

■ One famous **soliloquy** is Hamlet' speech that begins, "To be, or not to be . . ."

哈姆雷特最知名的**獨白**是：「生，抑或是死……」。

symbol 象徵

用以代表其他事物的人或物。

■ In Hawthorne's famous novel, the scarlet letter is a **symbol** for adultery.

在霍桑知名的小說中，紅字是姦淫罪的**象徵**。

theme 主題

戲劇或小說的主要意義；中心思想。

■ Ambition and revenge are common **themes** in Shakespeare's plays.

在莎士比亞的劇作中，雄心壯志與報復是常見的**主題**。

tragedy 悲劇

嚴肅且有悲傷結局的戲劇。

■ *Macbeth*, the shortest of Shakespeare's plays, is a **tragedy**.

莎士比亞最短的劇作《馬克白》是部**悲劇**。